ANGELS & IMPERFECTION

Angels & Imperfection Book 1

DAN ARNOLD

Angels & Imperfection
by Dan Arnold

Paperback Edition

CKN Christian Publishing
An Imprint of Wolfpack Publishing

6032 Wheat Penny Avenue
Las Vegas, NV 89122

Paperback ISBN: 978-1-64734-873-1
Ebook ISBN: 978-1-64734-872-4
Library of Congress Control Number: 2020935121

ANGELS & IMPERFECTION

DEDICATION

This book is dedicated to Lenora Clyde,
She was my faithful friend, fan, and the best
mother-in-law in the world. I miss you so. And to
Jake Arnold, Bart Arnold, Kelsey and Brett Collar,
Rachel Blevins and Loudin Blevins, all three of the
grandchildren - so far, Ellenor and Mike Welch,
Kathleen and Dave Golden, Bill Clyde (who has no
use for books and never read a page), and Al and
Andrea Kennemer, who have loved and encour-
aged me in the process.

And Lora,
My seldom complaining wife and travelling
companion as I explore this literary road in an
unreliable vehicle without a compass or GPS. She
pretends not to notice me trying to draw the map,
only after I've made all the wrong turns.

FOREWORD

"All we like sheep have gone astray."

Sheep are among the most naturally helpless inhabitants of this planet. Sheep are poorly equipped for either self-defense or rapid flight. When they are attacked, startled or frightened they tend to scatter.

Predators love helpless and harmless prey.

The most dangerous predators seek the lost sheep, not to harm them physically, but to herd them into darkness. Once in the darkness, the sheep are blind. Because lost sheep are blind, they will follow the whispered and gentle direction of any voice they feel comfortable with. The wolves entice them with pleasant and reasonable voices.

A smart predator gives the sheep just enough light, to follow the only path they can see, but not enough light to see the end of that path, or to see the traps and pitfalls along the way.

Other wolves will suggest the sheep are evolving into more enlightened beings; becoming more intelligent, perfect and godlike. Some will persuade the sheep there is no God, telling them that life is random and has no meaning whatsoever.

Since the dawn of time, the wolves have been determined to slaughter as many sheep as possible.

The Shepherds are appointed to stand between the sheep and the wolves.

CHAPTER 1

When I finally stumbled home at midnight, my next-door neighbor, Molly McGovern's lights were on. After the day I had just lived through, I was in no mood to put up with a lot of loud music, raucous laughter or any other form of inconsiderate behavior.

Like all people everywhere, Molly, was a flawed human being. That was no reason to abuse her. She was a drunk, sure, but that didn't mean her boyfriend had a license to use her as a punching bag.

As I climbed into bed I was only vaguely aware of my neighbors. I was awakened from a sound sleep by the noise of the beating. Through the wall of my apartment, I could hear the violence escalating.

I pulled on some pants and a T-shirt, and went out on the landing, barefooted.

I hesitated a moment before knocking.

Maybe I should just call the police again. They would show up in ten or twenty minutes. They might arrest Alphonsio Patterson again, but Molly probably wouldn't press charges, and he'd just go free... again. We'd all play the same scenario out again and again, just like we'd been doing for the last seven and a half months. Eventually, he would either kill her, leave her for another punching bag, or maybe Molly would kill him in his sleep. The restraining order wasn't doing anybody any good.

I pounded on the door.

A moment later, Alphonsio jerked it open. From the surprised look on his face I could tell he had been expecting the cops. When he recognized me, he went from startled to belligerent.

"What the F*** you want?"

"I was just wondering if I could borrow a cup of sugar."

"What? Hey, get the F*** outta here," he said, as I brushed past him into the living room.

"Can Molly come out and play?" I asked.

"You one crazy mothaf*****! I'm gonna **** you up."

I was aware Alphonsio had limited communication skills. Evidently this was due to a language barrier, based on his inability to express himself in words he had learned in school.

I ignored him and went into the bedroom. The door was open.

Molly was slumped in the corner, behind the bed. She was wearing green plaid pajama bottoms and a white tank top. The white tank top was slowly turning crimson, from the blood flowing out of Molly's broken nose and split lips. I went to her and found her semi-conscious and breathing. The once beautiful blonde woman was drunk and badly beaten.

"Get the f*** away from my girlfriend, mothaf*****!"

I stood up. "No, Al, my name is Tucker. I'm John Wesley Tucker."

Alphonsio was about my size, maybe a little taller. He was very fit, I could tell because he had no shirt on. He had several tattoos. Judging by the subject matter, poor quality of most of the artwork and my familiarity with his history, some of them were undoubtedly prison tats. He was wearing oversized blue jean cargo pants that were sagging down, exposing his boxer shorts. He had on a ball cap, sideways - one of those with a flat brim. I knew he was in his late twenties. Molly was thirty-two. They were both a bit younger than me, but then again, almost everyone is a bit younger than me.

I walked back into Molly's living room, in the apartment she paid the rent on.

"Alphonsio, I guess I'm going to have to call the police and an ambulance... again. Let me use your cell phone."

"What you say? Hell no. Get the F*** outta here."

I hit him, very hard and very fast. I hit him with the open heel of my right hand. I don't like to use my knuckles. The strike shattered his nose. I kicked him in the crotch, and followed it up with a left elbow strike, knocking him to the floor. He started to collect himself immediately, so I kicked him again. His head bounced off the corner of the breakfast bar and laid him out, stone cold. He looked to still be alive, and since he was lying face down, I knew he wouldn't drown in his own blood, from the broken nose.

I went over to a lamp that was lying on the floor, where it had been knocked over in his previous assault on Molly, and stripped the cord off. I used the cord to tie his hands behind his back.

Now I had a little time to think about what I should do next.

Molly needed medical attention. I would call for an ambulance, shortly.

First, I had to determine what to do with old Al.

The only thing I knew for sure was I didn't want him to ever touch Molly again.

It was nearly two in the morning, and nobody was moving outside. My apartment was second to the last, on the second story of the building. Molly's apartment was the last one, on the end, at the top of a staircase. I wanted to throw Alphonsio over the railing, and see if he survived the landing in the parking lot.

Maybe he would bounce.

I reminded myself he was some mother's little boy, her pride and joy. He was probably somebody's father. Maybe there was more than one child who could call him daddy. Above any other consideration, he was made in the image of God.

It only took me a couple of minutes of searching to find his dope stash. I knew he would have hidden it pretty quickly, when he thought the cops were at the door. I put it in his back pants pocket, sort of hanging out, where it could be seen, like his underwear. Then, I pulled out my cell phone and dialed 911.

I had just given the address to the dispatcher, when Alphonsio woke up, so I hung up the phone. He and I needed to chat before the police and the ambulance arrived on the scene.

I ducked into the kitchen and procured Molly's biggest cast iron frying pan.

Alphonsio had managed to sit up with his back against the breakfast bar, his legs bent in front of him.

He started to strain against the lamp cord, and tried to get up.

"Stop it," I said, brandishing the frying pan.

He quit squirming and glared at me. He looked kind of foolish, with the lower half of his face all bloody, like Molly's. I picked his cap off the floor, and put it back on his head, sideways, the way he liked to wear it.

"Alphonsio, I want you to listen to me for a second. The police are on the way here. I want you to promise me you will never come back to this apartment, and you will never see Molly again. OK?"

"F*** you," He responded.

I hit him in the right knee with the frying pan. I

hit him about as hard as I could. He nearly fainted, and crumpled over. I untied the lamp cord from around his wrists, and threw it back over in the corner, with the broken lamp. He was writhing on the floor, whimpering.

"Let's try this again, Alphonsio. I want you to promise me neither Molly, nor I, will ever see you again. OK?"

"You broke my knee, you motha…"

I broke his other knee.

He screamed this time, and then resumed writhing and whimpering in pain. I waited until he seemed to regain his wits.

"Well then, Al, since you appear to be unable to express yourself utilizing a normal vocabulary, let me put it to you another way. If I ever see you again, anytime, anywhere, I'll end you and send you to your final judgment. Nod your head if you understand."

He nodded vigorously, his whimpers punctuating the motion.

I carried the frying pan into the bedroom, where I handed it to Molly. She needed a little help getting a good grip on it. She was pretty much unaware she was holding it.

On my way out of the apartment, I checked on Alphonsio. He was still whimpering. He appeared somewhat paled and disheartened by the tribulation he had suffered.

I could hear sirens coming.

I left the apartment door open.

Yeah… I'm flawed, too.

CHAPTER 2

Spring time in East Texas, is often spectacular. This was one of those years, with the last of the redbuds just beginning to fade as the dogwoods came into full bloom. The air was fragrant, with azaleas and wisteria bursting with brightly colored blossoms. I decided to eat lunch outside.

The phone rang.

"Tucker Investigation, John speaking,"

"Mr. Tucker, please."

"Speaking."

"Are you John Wesley Tucker, the detective?"

"I am. May I ask who I'm speaking to?"

"I'm Walter Farley, Mr. Simpson's personal assistant. Please hold."

That was odd.

"Tucker, are you there?" a demanding voice boomed.

"Yes, sir, how may I help you?"

"I'm Ted Simpson, Simpson Oil and Gas, maybe you've heard of us."

"Yes, sir, I believe your offices are downtown, on the square. How may I help you, Mr. Simpson?"

"Can you come down here? I need to talk to you, privately. I'll buy you lunch."

"Let me check with my secretary to see if I have

any conflicts. Please hold."

I punched the "hold" button.

Tucker Investigations didn't have a secretary, yet, and I didn't have another appointment until three o'clock that afternoon. I just thought it would be fun to pretend. After all, turnabout is fair play.

I took him off hold.

"Mr. Simpson. It appears I can meet you for lunch. Where would you like to meet?"

"Come on down here, to the Simpson building. We'll talk first and then we'll eat."

He hung up.

The Simpson building was twelve stories of dark tinted glass, on the west side of the square, in downtown Tyler. Usually, it would only take me about ten minutes to get there. At lunch time, that driving time could nearly double. The lunch hour always causes a great migration. The downtown square is a popular destination for the hungry herd. There are some very good watering holes and grazing establishments on the square.

Because every parking space, anywhere near the square, was occupied, I had to park in the Episcopal Church parking lot, three blocks away.

I figured Mr. Simpson's office would be on the top floor of the Simpson Building, and so it was. I stepped off the elevator directly into a richly appointed reception area. A stunningly beautiful receptionist with flaming red hair was seated behind a massive lacquered walnut desk. She smiled as I approached.

"I'm John Wesley Tucker. I'm here to see Mr. Simpson."

"I believe he's expecting you, Mr. Tucker. Please have a seat."

She stood up from behind the desk and headed down the hall. I watched her go.

I barely had a minute to grab a business card off her desk, appreciate the tasteful décor and scan the covers of the glossy oil and gas industry magazines, before she returned.

"He'll see you in just a moment."

"Thank you, ma'am," I said, with a smile.

I sat down in a giant arm chair, upholstered in black and white speckled cowhide, with big brass nail head trim. After a moment, a man appeared at the end of the hall. He looked to be in his early thirties. He stood about five nine and weighed about a buck eighty. He was wearing black pants below an open neck, black polo shirt. He was in no big hurry, and stopped to speak to someone in another office as he approached.

"Mr. Tucker, I'm Walter Farley. I'm Mr. Simpson's personal assistant. We spoke on the phone."

We shook hands.

"I'll show you to his office."

Ted Simpson's personal workspace was a corner office with a spectacular view of Tyler. I was reminded immediately of why I love this city so much. The view suggested a forest with the occasional church steeple rising through it. In some places though, the bank buildings were taller than the steeples.

As we came in, Mr. Simpson was coming around his desk to meet us. He was about six feet tall, a little on the heavy side, with salt and pepper hair, neatly trimmed. He wore an expensive dark grey suit, over a pale blue shirt with a white collar and a tie of deep blue silk. He had on black tasseled loafers. He looked ready to pose for Forbes or Gentleman's Quarterly.

"Ted, this is John Wesley Tucker. Mr. Tucker this is Ted Simpson." Walter introduced me, as if he knew me personally. I shook hands with Mr.

Simpson and he directed me to have a seat in front of his desk.

Walter asked if I would like coffee, which I declined.

"I know you're wondering why I wanted to meet with you," Mr. Simpson started.

Actually, I was wondering if Walter was going to stay for the "private" meeting.

He was.

"I have a situation that requires some delicacy. I understand you can be trusted, and you get the job done." Mr. Simpson said.

"May I ask who recommended me, to you?"

He looked at Walter.

"Let's just say that you have a reputation," Walter said.

"I would prefer to think I have references or referrals."

"Whatever, let's get down to brass tacks," Mr. Simpson said.

The upshot of it all was Ted Simpson was planning to run for state office. He wanted me to do a simple investigation, to see if I could find any dirt, or potentially embarrassing incident from his past, which his enemies could use against him. It didn't mean there actually was dirt, but it did mean they wanted an independent investigator to take a look. This was a fairly routine and sensible practice. It was certain his opponents would conduct their own investigations.

"My fee structure is simple, Mr. Simpson. I charge $450.00 per day, plus expenses. My day rate does not imply that I will spend all day, every day, on your case. I have other clients. I will provide you with a written account of my efforts and findings. I will also invoice you and provide receipts for the expenses."

"No, I don't need any written records. Walter will give you $5,000.00 as a retainer. That should cover one week's worth of work and expenses. I probably won't see you again, after today. Walter will check in with you from time to time, you can let him know your progress. Do we have a deal?"

I hesitated. Aside from his aggressive approach, there was something about all of this that rubbed me the wrong way.

"Mr. Simpson, how should I say this... there might be something that comes up, which you and I need to discuss. That discussion might not need to include your personal assistant. No offense, Walter."

Walter looked sort of surprised.

I saw the wheels turning in Mr. Simpson's head.

"Yeah, well I don't anticipate that happening. But in case it does, Walter will give you my private number. Don't call me unless it's damned important. Now then, is it a deal or no deal?" He held out his hand.

I shook it.

"Good. Let's get some lunch," Mr. Simpson said.

To my surprise, we walked right across the hall, to another corner room with a spectacular view of the city. This space was appointed as a banquet area. There were buffet tables with a variety of delicacies from breads to meats, side dishes, even desserts. The dining table had a sparkling white table cloth with an elaborate, low, arrangement of fresh flowers. There were crystal goblets, wine glasses, and silverware, even linen napkins.

"Grab you a plate, Mr. Tucker. James will be here in a moment to get your drink order. I'd try that blackened prime rib, if I was you."

We enjoyed a delightful lunch. We were joined by a couple of other Simpson Oil and Gas employees, to whom I was introduced simply as, Mr. Tucker. I was pretty much ignored, as the conversation shifted from business trivialities to current NFL football highlights. Evidently, Mr. Simpson was a Dallas Cowboys fan.

After lunch, Walter took me to his office, where he handed me a large manila envelope, with $5,000.00 in cash in it. It held fifty, one hundred dollar bills, bundled into five stacks, with ten bills in each stack, the very definition of a tidy sum. He also handed me a business card for Simpson Oil and Gas, with no personalized name on it. Two phone numbers were hand printed on the back.

"The top number is my personal cell phone. The bottom number is Mr. Simpson's private line. Don't call him, unless I tell you that you can."

I figured I would make my own decisions about who I called and when.

He walked me to the elevator.

"Nice to meet you, Mr. Tucker, keep me informed. I'll be seeing you." He walked away.

As the elevator doors were closing, I looked over at the receptionist.

She gave me a dazzling smile.

CHAPTER 3

My three o'clock appointment was going to be unpleasant, at best. I would rather have had an appointment for a root canal, or even a colonoscopy. This meeting was likely to be more painful and uncomfortable than either of those, on several levels.

Mr. and Mrs. Robert Winslow, 'Bob and Sandy', wanted me to investigate the disappearance of their 10 year old daughter, Victoria.

I had seen the story on the news.

Mrs. Winslow had left her daughter in the car, doing her homework, while she went into the supermarket. When she came out with the groceries, Victoria was gone. At first Sandy figured Victoria (she hated to be called Vicky) had just followed her into the store, so she went looking for her. She had the store manager page her. The store manager sent employees searching for her. Sandy started to come unglued and became hysterical. The manager called the police.

The police determined Victoria was not in the store, her mother's car, or the parking lot. They reviewed the video tape from the surveillance cameras.

The parking lot cameras had recorded an average-sized man, in a hoodie sweatshirt with the hood pulled up, wandering through the parking lot, kind of looking under cars near Sandy's vehicle. He was seen approaching Sandy's car and engaging Victoria in conversation.

Victoria got out of the car and went with the man to look under other cars. They disappeared from view. Neither Sandy nor Bob (who had been called in from work), had any idea who the man in the video images might be.

After the search of the surrounding neighborhoods by the police, friends, and volunteers, after all the usual investigation and interviews of known offenders, after grilling members of the family and all the friends of the family, even after the video tape was shown on the local and national news channels, the police had nothing.

My friend, Detective Sergeant Tony Escalante of the Tyler PD, had told the family, I might be able to help.

It had been nearly a week since the little girl went missing.

"I know Tony Escalante recommended me to you, but the police have done a very thorough investigation. I don't want to take y'all's money and end up telling you the same thing they did. I'm so sorry, but in a case like this, there is seldom a happy ending. We just don't have any real leads to follow," I said.

"I don't care what it costs. We'll mortgage the house. We have to know what has happened to our little girl," Bob said.

Sandy just sat there, crying.

"I understand completely, but I don't want to benefit from your tragedy. I'll do what I can. I'll do some investigating and I'll pray for you, and for her. I can't make any promises beyond that. In the meantime, it would probably be best, if you just concentrate on remembering Victoria as happy and healthy. I'll give you the name of my pastor; he's excellent at counseling folks in a crisis."

"We want you to help us find our daughter, please help us," Sandy Winslow sobbed.

"We'll pay you a retainer," Bob added.

I held up my hands.

"Please, Mr. Winslow, I don't want your money. I told you, I'll do what I can, but I can't promise you anything."

"Business is business." Bob said, as he wrote out a check. "This is to secure your services, not as payment for anything certain. Maybe having to earn the money will provide additional motivation."

He handed me the check. It was made out to me, for one thousand dollars.

I said thank you, and put it in my pocket. I had no intention of ever cashing it.

The next morning, Tony called me.

"Did you take that job for Mr. and Mrs. Winslow?"

"Not exactly, Tony. I told them I would look into it, but there is very little chance I can help."

"Can you shoot this evening?"

I knew by "shoot," he meant meet him at the shooting range, where we practiced.

"OK. I'll meet you there."

When I entered the indoor range, Tony was already set up in a shooting lane. He had reserved the next station for me. There was no one else there.

When I arrived at Tony's shooting station, he looked grim.

"Hey, J.W., how's it going?"

"Super, how are you?"

"I have good days and bad days."

I nodded, and then I asked him.

"Have you made any progress on the missing child case?"

He shook his head.

"Not really, but now we have this."

He reached into a pocket inside his jacket and removed a plastic sleeve, with a Polaroid photo in it.

"This morning we got a call from a citizen at the supermarket where the Winslow girl disappeared. We sent a uniform over there, and this is what the person found lying in the parking lot."

He passed me the plastic sleeve.

"We checked out the citizen and she's clean. We ran the photo for prints and did a battery of tests. The lady who found the photo has her prints on it, and there are other partials."

I looked at the picture. Then I started studying it.

"Were any of the partials enough to get a match?"

"Apparently not, we thought maybe so, but not one of them was complete enough. We didn't get a hit from any of the data bases."

"I didn't know you could still get Polaroid film. How old is it? How long do you think it may have been lying out there?"

"The techs say the picture is only a couple of days old. It wasn't out in the elements for long. It hadn't been run over, and it wasn't blown into the parking lot by the wind. It hasn't been faded by the sun. They think it was probably dropped there last night or this morning."

"... Nothing on the surveillance cameras?" I asked.

He shook his head, as his only response.

"Why are you showing this to me?"

"We've done everything we can do with it. It's just information, another dead end."

I took a long slow breath. I wished he hadn't phrased it that way.

"Have you tried to get a match on the car's make, model and year?"

He nodded and said, "We haven't been able to get anything firm. It's probably American, maybe a nineties vintage, maybe newer, maybe not - like I said, nothing for sure. I'll ask the FBI if they can identify it from the photograph." He shrugged.

"Have you shown this to the Winslow's yet?"

"I don't want to, but I'm supposed to. You know, to get a positive ID. Matches the description and the other photos they provided us exactly, though."

"What do you know about the other one?"

"Hard to tell from the photo, we might have a lead, but I can't discuss it with you, yet."

"As disturbing as this is, it's kind of encouraging at the same time."

"How's that, J.W.?"

"Victoria was taken nearly a week ago. The picture was probably dropped here deliberately. The perp may still be in the area."

He nodded.

"Yeah, but only you could see something positive in that."

"There's something else even more significant."

"What's that?"

I handed the Polaroid back to Tony

"These kids were both alive when this picture was taken."

The photo showed two children lying in the trunk of a car. They were bound and had been gagged with duct tape.

From the pictures I had seen and the video of the abduction, I could see the girl was clearly Victoria Winslow. The boy was younger and smaller than Victoria. She was lying in front of him, partly obscuring him. The duct tape over his mouth covered most of the whole lower half of his face.

I felt the old anger at the evil permeating and perverting humanity and poisoning this world. It helped me focus on my shooting. I chose my favourite .45 and set the target at fifteen yards. Tony was shooting his service Sig .40. He started at fifteen yards also.

We both fired fifty rounds. We both shot well.

Out in the parking lot, I looked at Tony and said, "We both know that's Victoria Winslow in the photo, right?"

He nodded silently in response.

"Do you really have to show the picture to the Winslow family?"

Tony opened the trunk of his car to put his gun bag into it. We both stood there, looking into the empty trunk.

"No," he said. "I don't believe I will."

CHAPTER 4

Ted Simpson had inherited his interest in Simpson Oil and Gas from his father, Gus Simpson. Ted's father had likewise inherited his father's oil and gas interests. All three generations had managed the business with ruthless precision, making Simpson Oil and Gas the leading independent producer in North America. Simpson Oil and Gas, Ted in particular, had recognized the value of emerging technologies, and they led the way in the most innovative and effective horizontal drilling, hydraulic fracturing, completions and production techniques.

At one point, by acquiring millions of acres of leasehold in several states, they managed to corner the market on nearly every major natural gas play in North America.

Unfortunately, Ted had over-extended his credit and his investor's money in the process. He had almost singlehandedly eliminated the formerly normal cyclic supply shortages. Now there was a glut of available natural gas. The storage facilities were flooded, but because demand had not increased, the market price of natural gas had plummeted.

Ted was forced to sell off much of their land

holdings in leases, in several states. He had to sell some of the corporate stock as well. His timing was excellent and he saved the company, putting it back on secure and profitable footing.

Many of the assets were sold to foreign investors, most notably investors from China and Saudi Arabia. This made him unpopular with some folks, but probably would not be a deal killer for his election dreams.

I could find nothing in his business life that would be seen as scandalous.

Personally, he had an unpleasant reputation for putting money ahead of the people in his life. For him, turning a tidy profit came before any other consideration. At worst he appeared to be greedy to a fault. He lived for the profit. Usually, his shareholders benefitted from this mind set. His family and employees did not. Still, it was nothing that would pose a serious threat to an election campaign.

Politically, he had contributed money to candidates running in both parties. He was said to be a fiscal conservative and a social liberal. He could afford to finance his own campaign, but he had long standing connections with powerful people he could use for fund raising. He was very good at using people. If an election could be bought, he would buy it.

I was thinking about these things, when the phone rang.

"Mr. Tucker, this is Walter Farley. I was wondering if you've made any progress in your enquiries."

"I've done some research into Mr. Simpson's business history and practices."

"I see. I'd like to hear your thoughts on what you've found. May I come by your office?"

"Certainly, Mr. Farley, when would you like to

make an appointment?"

"Well… now - right now. In fact, I'll be there in a minute."

I didn't like it.

"No, wait, that…" He had hung up.

That did it. I realized it was time to get a secretary. I needed somebody to protect me from free-roaming jackasses.

"… So, to sum up, there is nothing scandalous or clearly egregious in his business history or practices. I'd say he is going to have a hard time selling the idea he is both a social progressive and a fiscal conservative. You can't be supportive of liberal social programs, and at the same time, deny them funding." I concluded.

"We really aren't interested in your political opinion, Mr. Tucker," Walter said. "We hired you to investigate whether or not there's anything Mr. Simpson's enemies might be able to use against him."

"I had to start somewhere. I chose to explore his business life, first. I'll get into other areas as I go along. You are aware Mr. Simpson represents 'Big Oil' in the minds of many average Texas voters? If there was something Simpson Oil and Gas had done and covered up, I needed to find out. Even a serious environmental issue could kill his political aspirations."

"I see your point. Are you confident you have eliminated those concerns?"

I nodded and replied, "Yep, there's nothing there that could be used to do any serious harm to him or his campaign. Y'all are already addressing the environmental issues and concerns associated with hydraulic fracturing. I'm aware certain celebrities have protested and chained themselves to trees, but the Texas Railroad Commission has no beef with Simpson Oil and Gas, and the EPA hasn't been able to prove any of the claims about contaminated well water. There are numerous studies showing methane contamination has occurred often throughout history, and continues to occur naturally, drilling or no drilling. It appears the incidents that actually have been directly linked to drilling are about casing issues in the vertical bores, unrelated to hydraulic fracturing. The stories do get a lot of media attention though, don't they?"

He shook his head.

"Again, that's not your concern. Move on. What will your investigative skills be applied to next?"

Now, I found his attitude… unacceptable.

Opening my desk drawer, I took out the big manila envelope full of money.

Walter appeared to have a smirk on his face.

I opened the envelope and looked inside.

"Ok. It's all still here." I observed.

Looking over at Walter, I tossed the whole thing in his lap.

Evidently my unexpected move made Walter angry. His face turned beet-red.

"There's your money, Walter. Since I haven't performed to your exacting standards, you can get someone else to handle the job."

I stood up, to show Walter to the door.

"Now hold on, Mr. Tucker. We seem to have gotten off on the wrong foot. There's no need for you to be petty about this."

"Be careful, Walter. I don't like to be insulted, especially while I'm standing in my own office."

He nodded, but stayed seated.

"Very well, I apologize. I didn't intend any insult. Can we start over? I fear I've managed this badly." He said.

"That's exactly the point, Walter. If you want to manage my work, you'll have to give better directions. No, on second thought, I don't care to have you manage my work, at all. Take the money back to Mr. Simpson, and tell him that for me."

Walter was not happy. I could see he was working hard at trying to maintain his temper, his composure and his dignity.

I really didn't care about any of those things.

"Again, Mr. Tucker, I apologize. You are quite correct. It's not my place to criticize your efforts. The work you have done so far has been quite thorough. Please excuse my error."

Wow, I hadn't expected this response. He had to swallow a big chunk of his personal pride, to say all that.

I took a deep breath.

"OK, we did get off on the wrong foot. That's partly my fault. I didn't ask Mr. Simpson for any direction. Is there something specific you want me to look for?"

"No, no. I appreciate that you must employ your own methods. I wouldn't be able to direct the efforts of the opposition, either. Please proceed as you think best."

As he stood up, he put the envelope back on my desk.

"I trust I can tell Mr. Simpson you are continuing with your investigations?"

"Sure. I'm on the case." I smiled.

He didn't return the smile. He moved very stiffly to the door. I could tell I had offended him.

I almost felt bad about that.

After he left, I wondered why he hadn't just gone to another agency. Other agencies had more man-power and could gather information more quickly.

It was odd. I had offended Walter, yet he still wanted me to investigate.

Why?

Evidently, Walter was a small part of a bigger picture, but I had no idea what it was. At this point, his involvement was like a single piece to a jigsaw puzzle. Other pieces were missing, and there was no image on the box lid.

CHAPTER 5

"… No, I think your deposition and the video you provided will be all that's required. It went very well and covered all the bases. I doubt we'll even have to put you on the stand. I think it's a slam dunk, John. He'll do time, for sure. Thanks for all your hard work. Send us your invoice."

This was apparently the satisfactory end of an insurance fraud case I had worked.

"You bet. Thank you, Gwen. Call if you need me."

In this case, the guy had almost managed to swindle a personal fortune out of the insurance company, which you and I would have had to pay for in higher premiums. Instead, he would soon be on his way to prison.

I drove back to the scene where Victoria Winslow had been taken. On a previous visit, I'd started by observing the supermarket from a distance, at the same time of day Victoria had disappeared, watching the traffic patterns and the ebb and flow of customers. Standing where Sandy Winslow had parked her car, I headed off on foot in the same direction Victoria and the perp had gone, as they disappeared from the store's video image. I hadn't learned anything very useful on that first visit except investigating the location convinced me the kidnapper must have had a car somewhere nearby.

Today, I was trying to figure where the kidnapper had parked his car. It had to be somewhere fairly close, but not so exposed someone would have noticed him taking the girl. If he had put the girl into his car in the parking lot, someone would have seen it, and it would have appeared in the surveillance video.

The supermarket was located on south Broadway, the busiest street in Tyler, at one of the busiest intersections. It was a commercial hub, with big box stores and restaurants all around, only half a block from the Broadway Square shopping mall to the north and a strip mall to the south.

All that traffic, but no one had reported seeing anything. The media had let Sandy plead for information. The police, and the news anchors continued to request that anyone who saw anything remotely suspicious on the day of the abduction, call in. There had not been one useful report.

I was now persuaded whoever had done this was a local person. Someone randomly passing through the area could not have planned this so well.

That was the key.

I started thinking about how I would have done it.

Evidently the perp had used the old trick of pretending to look for a lost pet. Kids always wanted to help look for the lost kitty or puppy. It had worked on Victoria. He must have done this before.

I found myself standing in the parking lot of the strip mall, only a half block south of the supermarket. There was a spot here where a car could have been parked and no one driving by would have noticed it. There were no video cameras here. This was where I would have parked. I would have backed into the space, putting the back of my vehicle within two or three feet of a high wall that wrapped around an apartment complex. The car could not been seen from the apartments.

As I considered these things, I felt I was being watched. There was a very tall and thin, black man, standing in the narrow space between the wall of the apartment complex and the wall of the strip mall, about 50 feet away.

He had a shopping cart with him. I remembered there was a homeless man who routinely travelled around this area. I'd seen him frequently over the last few months. This might be the same man.

Could he have taken the girl?

It was highly unlikely, for a number of reasons, not the least of which was he was not the man in the images on the video tape. I knew nothing at all about him. I decided to try to approach him.

He was waiting for me, with a big smile!

"You that angel, Good Angel," he said.

"My name is John Wesley Tucker. What's your name?"

"You not the bad angel," he replied, with a frown.

"I'm John. What's your name?"

"They say I'm Dustin. My cart is rustin', when I dance I'm bustin'!" He did kind of a rolling wave movement starting with his right hand, up the arm, over his shoulders and down the other arm. He ended by pushing his face to one side, with his left hand. He rolled his eyes and laughed.

I laughed too.

"Hello, Dustin, where do you live?"

"I live here, I live there, I be livin' everywhere!"

It was apparent he had all his worldly possessions in the shopping cart. There was even a bible on the little shelf by the push handle.

He saw me looking at the bible.

"He told me you was comin'. He say you help. He say you a good angel."

"Who told you that, Dustin?"

He looked up at the sky and closed his eyes.

"Our Father. He say you come to help her."

"Dustin, look at me."

He looked me in the eye.

"Who am I supposed to help?"

"It was the bad angel done it, he that took her."

"Dustin, did you talk to the police?"

"Uh huh. When it gets cold, they come get me," he replied.

I thought for a moment. This could be just the confused ramblings of a troubled mind. Maybe he had seen something happen here, or maybe he had just been told about it.

"Did something happen to a little girl?"

He looked away and choked a little. "The bad angel hit her and put her in his car."

He had my full attention now. This was going to require careful questioning.

"What car, Dustin?"

"It was like the sky, and it had a reindeer."

What did that mean? Like the sky...?

"Was it a blue car?

I regretted the question immediately. I was suggesting things to him, not asking questions of him.

"You stupid for an angel," he snorted.

I decided to try a different line of questions.

"Tell me about the bad angel."

He shook his head.

"It's not my war, you the one that gots to deal with him."

I thought some more.

"Tell me about the reindeer."

"It was flying, over a silver football."

What did that mean? Was the silver football some kind of Dallas Cowboys emblem? Their colors were blue and silver. On the other hand, everyone knows the Cowboy's logo is a star, not a football or a reindeer.

"Where was the car?"

He pointed to where I had been standing a few moments ago.

"I got to go on now, I got me my rounds"

He started to push his cart up the narrow little alley.

"When did you see the bad angel?" I called.

"Last time he was here. When he took the girl," he said, walking away.

CHAPTER 6

"Come on, J.W.," Tony reasoned. "He's been questioned by at least three different patrol officers and one detective. The day Victoria Winslow was taken; he was interviewed as a possible suspect. He just babbled nonsense and clammed up. You know how it is with some of these homeless vagrants. They get off their meds and get all confused. It's been nearly a week since the girl disappeared. He probably wants to help, but he doesn't know anything."

"He saw something, Tony. I'm sure of it. He put the car exactly where I would have expected it to be. How could he know that? How could he even know we're looking for a car? We didn't know ourselves, until a couple of days ago when the photo turned up. No one could have told him."

Tony sat thoughtfully for a moment.

"You may be right, but flying reindeer and footballs aren't much help. Are we supposed to put out a BOLO for an unknown make and model of car, a car that might be blue, with some sort of football symbol on it? This is Texas. How many vehicles with football emblems do you think we could find, in about ten minutes?"

"I understand. I'm just letting you know what I've learned so far."

He nodded.

"Appreciate that. I'll do the same for you."

"You have something?"

He sighed, "It's about the little boy in the photo. His name is probably Aaron Horowitz. A little boy by that name appears to have been abducted from his back yard, near Marshall, Texas, four days ago. His parents thought he was playing in their fenced back yard, but when they called him in for dinner, he was gone. They figured he'd left the yard to go play in the woods. They live in a neighborhood that backs up to some deep woods. When they couldn't find him, they called the Harrison County Sheriff's department. A search was organized, but they found nothing. There has never been a clue." Tony continued, "Here's the thing, J.W. The little boy in the Polaroid matches the description they gave us. I sent a scanned image to the Harrison County Sheriff's department this morning. Mr. and Mrs. Horowitz were shown the photo. They say it is Aaron, their son."

"Awwwwhh!" I groaned.

"Yeah, I know. I'm right there with you," Tony said.

"Marshall is a long way from here. I wonder what the connection is."

"All we have so far is the boy was abducted from near Marshall, and the girl was abducted from Tyler. Both were seen together in a photo, lying in a car trunk. The photo was found in the same parking lot where the girl was last seen. That's it, and that's all. We really don't have any leads."

My investigation into Ted Simpson's life had revealed he had attended a public high school, not a fancy, private prep school. It was a bit unusual for the uber-wealthy, not what I would've expected.

At fifteen, he had gotten a "hardship" driving permit, even though his family's mansion was only about ten blocks from the public high school he attended. It was odd, of course, but it was merely amusing, not scandalous.

When I interviewed some of the locals who had known him in high school, they all said he was just a normal teenager. While he was involved in some of the social activities that were, more or less the exclusive realm of the wealthy he had never seemed to be arrogant or boastful. He always drove a pickup truck. A fancy, lifted and tricked out 4X4 pickup, but a pickup all the same. He enjoyed hunting and fishing, water skiing, and ATV riding. These were all pretty typical interests for teenage boys in Tyler, Texas.

After high school he attended Texas A&M University, where he earned a bachelor's degree in petroleum engineering. I had more research to do on his college years.

I was stopped at a red light, talking to Walter on my cell phone about Mr. Simpson's high school days, when I noticed the chrome on the car ahead of me.

"Walter, something's come up. I'll have to call you back."

I hung up on him and called Tony, as the light changed.

"Detective Escalante here, what can I do for you?" he answered.

"Tony, it could be a Chevy Impala."

"J.W., how in the world did you find out? I just got an e-mail with photo attachments, from the FBI. They've concluded the car trunk is almost certainly that of a late model Chevrolet, probably an Impala. The trunk photos look to be an exact match."

"I'm driving on Loop 323, right behind a bright red Impala. Do you remember the Impala emblem? There was usually one on the trunk, and one on each side, of older models."

"Kind of, I guess. Why?"

"It's a bright silver piece of chrome. It's a leaping impala, a type of African antelope, but it kind of looks like a reindeer, flying over or through, an oval, shaped more or less like a football."

"Good grief. You figured it out from a piece of chrome?"

"Tony, this proves Dustin saw the car. He saw the kidnapping!"

"I'll have him picked up for further questioning."

"No, don't do that. If he gets scared, he'll shut-down."

"We have to talk to him, J.W., he's the one, single, and only lead we have." Tony was adamant.

"Right, locate him, Tony, but don't interfere with him or try to apprehend him. Call me, and I'll go wherever he is. He might talk to me, but not if he's been hauled downtown by policemen."

"That's no good, J.W. I'll have to interview him. This is official police business. I can't use sec-ond-hand information."

He was right.

"Then we'll talk to him together, Tony. Just you and I, but we'll go to him. Don't have him dragged downtown."

I could hear the wheels grinding in Detective Anthony Escalante's head, even over a cell phone. It took a long time for the wheels to grind to a halt.

"OK. I'll bet several of our patrol officers know his usual haunts. I'll have him located and I'll call you. We'll go interview him together."

That's the thing about Tony; he's pretty regimented in his approach to his work. He tries to do every-thing by the book, all the time.

Tony believes adherence to the rules and regulations helps to ensure and enforce justice. Without the rules and regulations, those who serve in law enforcement could all too easily abuse their power.

I respect his position on the matter.

It annoys the fire out of me, though.

CHAPTER 7

Molly had been home from the hospital for a couple of days, but I hadn't seen her. This evening, she was standing on the landing, smoking a cigarette, with a glass of Vodka in her hand.

"Johnny, did you call the police on Alphonsio? They got him in the hospital for parole violations." She slurred.

She was a bit confused

"Hi, Molly, How are you?"

She made several faces. One face was sad, another angry, the next was confused. She ended on happy. She smiled. "Hi Johnny, I'm good. How are you?"

"I'm happy to see you."

Both her eyes were blackened. Her face was swollen and colorful. Her nose was taped.

"You're so good to me, Johnny. Give me a kiss."

She puckered up her split lips, but I kissed her on the forehead. Even her hair reeked of vodka, and cigarette smoke.

Molly had been beautiful once. I hoped that one day, she would be again. Here, or there.

She was drinking herself to death.

***

Life on earth is hard. In some locations, the environment is so extreme, just living through a day can be tortuous. For many the hardships are not environmental, they are emotional, psychological or physiological. People do things they should not do.

It's not my place to judge. We all have a judge. We'll all face Him, soon enough.

Until then, some of us are called to speak the truth, in love.

Sometimes, truth hurts.

The darkness hates the truth.

We are called to be salt, and light.

The darkness hates the light.

Salt preserves that which is good, it also gives flavor.

The darkness corrupts everything, and the darkness hates our flavor.

We can't save the lost. They have a Saviour.

We can love them, though. We can lead them to the Saviour. Sometimes, that is all we can do. What they choose to do after that, is beyond our mission, or our control.

"Molly, do you want to get better? Would you like to be sober?"

She made some more faces.

It's pretty much pointless to talk to someone while they're drunk.

She sort of smiled, a sad smile, and nodded her head.

"We'll talk tomorrow. I know of a program through our church, which can help you."

Inside my apartment, I called Christine Valakova. She was the red headed receptionist at Simpson Oil and Gas.

I had called her earlier in the week, to make a date.

"You still want sushi?" I asked.

"Oh yeah, with ginger and wasabi, and red wine," she added.

"OK, I'll pick you up at 6:30."

Tyler is the regional center for the professional occupations, medical, banking, legal, and a host of others. The city attracts students to the University of Texas at Tyler, Tyler Junior College, and other colleges.

Tyler has most of the amenities of a big city, while retaining a small town atmosphere. If the traffic is light, you can drive from one side to the other, in about twenty minutes. Tyler is known as the Rose City or the Rose Capital of the U.S.; because most of all the roses sold in this country, are processed, or are produced in and around Tyler, Texas.

The only Tyler rose I was interested in tonight, was Christine Valakova.

I picked her up at her apartment. It was in an upscale, gated apartment complex. Her apartment was beautiful. She had decorated it in warm jewel and earth tones. She told me she had been living alone for a couple of months, since her roommate had moved out.

Tonight she wore a green dress that could have been tailored to fit her. It had some sort of sparkly crystals and sequins on the bodice. She had a necklace and earrings, also made of sparkly crystals that flashed changing colors in the light.

She introduced me to her cat whose name was Mr. Tumescence, although she always called him "Tummy" or "Tum Tum." She explained that when she named him, she thought that the word meant "Fat."

Go figure.

We headed to the trendy sushi place, best known for the creative and colorful preparation and presentation, by an award winning chef.

"… My family name goes back to some of the people called Romani who traveled throughout Europe, without any particular national allegiance," she said.

You could have knocked me over with a feather!

"My grandfather was a leader among the Romani here in America, back at the end of the nineteenth century," I said.

"We could be related," we both said, together at the same time.

We both laughed, and I asked her, "How did you end up here in East Texas?"

She was pensive for a moment.

"My boyfriend in college was from here. We were going to get married, or so he said. After I graduated, I moved here to be with him. He's gone to Chicago now, and married to someone else. I'm still here."

She made a face.

"Where's your family?" I asked

"They're mostly in the hill country, just northwest of Austin. My brother and his family live in Dallas."

"What about your family?" she asked

"I'm all there is. The end of the line, I was an only child."

"Where are your parents?"

"They were killed in a tornado in Oklahoma, several years ago, while I was in the Navy."

"How long were you in the Navy?"

I figured I should restrict my answer to the most recent term of service.

"Eight years. I probably would have made a career of it, the Navy that is, but I got hurt and some other things happened that sort of ended my interest."

"What do you do now?" she asked.

That question posed a problem. She didn't know

that I was working for her boss.

"After the Navy I went to work for the Department of Homeland Security. Eventually, I got tired of the system and the politics. There were too many layers of bureaucracy. I came back here and went to work for myself. I own my own business"

"Doing what?"

"I do private investigation."

"Really, a P.I., like on TV?"

I get that a lot.

"Well, no, not really. I drive a pickup, not a Ferrari or anything. I help families in crisis and locate missing heirs, that sort of thing, and I provide services to attorneys and corporate clients. It tends to be kind of boring and tedious work, mostly"

"Wow," she said. "I kind of figured you for a security type. I knew you weren't one of those goons Walter uses, but you have a certain air about you."

"Goons?"

What was she talking about?

"Oh, I'm sorry. I didn't mean you look like a goon, or anything... uh, I just meant that you don't act like a typical, pot-bellied, business type."

I must have looked exasperated, but I was really only amused and a little perplexed.

"OH! I really am sorry. I know you own your own business. I just meant..." She trailed off, dismally.

I laughed.

"It's OK. I get that a lot. People are always asking me if I'm in law enforcement."

She looked relieved.

"That's it. That's what I meant. Do you carry a gun?"

"Yes, I do. Not always, of course, but usually."

"Why, what are you afraid of?"

"When I have my gun, I'm not afraid of much of anything."

We both smiled, and drank some wine.

Eventually, I asked her about Walter's "goons".

"Mr. Simpson never travels without his security people. Walter hires them, and I think he scrapes the bottom of the barrel. Oh, I'll bet they're plenty competent. They manage to be big and scary, very well. They have the whole intimidation thing locked down. They just lack class."

"What do you mean?" I asked.

"They're all stamped from the same mold. You know, former football jocks, ex-military, swaggering, cocky, adolescent, locker room, baboons."

She rolled her eyes.

"Have you had problems with them?" I asked.

"Every single one of them has hit on me. They're vulgar and disgusting. Walter seems to think it's funny. I am not amused."

I nodded.

"Yeah, I can see that."

"I am so sorry if I indicated I thought you were like one of those guys."

"Not a problem, Christine." I smiled.

We both enjoyed dinner and being together.

CHAPTER 8

Something happened in college. Ted Simpson left A&M early one semester. He didn't drop out of school and he didn't fail any classes. He returned to the university the next semester and finished college with a respectable GPA. Why had he left College Station early that semester? Where did he go? There was a trail here, a hidden trail.

There had been no illness in his family. He hadn't reported any illness of his own to the school. Had his father sent for him? The classmates I interviewed only told me they all knew he had left. If they knew why, they weren't talking. I was still trying to find his former roommate. I also wanted to interview his current roommate, his wife of twenty five years, Corinne Simpson.

I was following still another trail with regard to the "goons" Walter employed as security.

Christine had been right. Ted Simpson never travelled without a security escort. Because I did the occasional personal security job myself. I was familiar with a variety of possible threats, and did potential threat assessments for some of my corporate clients. I could understand his need for personal security, if he were traveling in a third world country, where kidnapping or murder was a very real and constant threat, but why do so in the U.S.? What or who was he afraid of? What was Walter's connection to this? The more I dug, the more questions I had.

Another question nagging at me was why hadn't the police found Dustin? He was pretty easy to spot, pushing his shopping cart along. Of course it was possible other things interfered with the BOLO. It only meant "be on the lookout." Unless they were seriously looking for a suspect in a specific crime, a lost Alzheimer's patient, or something that posed an actual danger to the public a BOLO was sort of an "oh by the way" for the street cops. If Dustin had robbed a bank, or if he were a loose tiger, they would be looking more intently. These things would be cause for an "all points" bulletin.

My phone rang. It was my personal cell phone, not my office phone or the other mobile phone. I looked at the caller I.D.

"Hey, Christine, how are you?"

"I'm pissed!"

"Excuse me?"

"I've had it. Now it's Walter who's hitting on me."

"Oh. I'm sorry to hear that."

I was wondering why she was calling me about a personal problem at her place of employment.

"He said he knew I had gone out with you, and what I needed was a 'real' man, with a 'real' job."

I sighed. I had no appropriate words in response.

"So, that's it. I quit." She stated.

"Now hold on, it's never a good idea to quit a job, unless or until you have another one lined up."

"You sound like my father. I don't care. I'd rather wait tables than work in that place. I told Walter he could find another receptionist."

And there it was. I needed a receptionist. Christine needed a job. How very convenient for everyone, right?

Maybe it was a little too convenient.

How had Walter known Christine and I had gone out? Did Christine tell him? Would Walter like to have a spy in my office? Suddenly Christine was available.

Good grief! I was turning completely paranoid. I might as well be schizophrenic too.

"Are you still there, in the Simpson building?" I asked her.

"No, Walter became very angry. He called me some names I won't repeat. I told him he could go to hell. He had one of his security goons escort me out."

She sounded like she was about to cry.

"OK, Christine, can you come here, to my office?"

"Sure, where is it?"

I gave her directions.

"I'll be there in about fifteen minutes," she said, and hung up.

The first time I called her, to ask her out, I called the number on her card, which I had picked up at her desk. It said "Christine Valakova, Liaison." I found it an amusing title for a receptionist to put on a business card. Later, she gave me her personal cell phone number.

Did Walter have a way of knowing the content of every call coming into that office? Did he monitor Christine's cell phone? Where had the "security goon" come from? There was no security desk at the Simpson building. Anyone could walk in off the street, get in the elevator, punch a button and walk right into Ted Simpson's office. Stopping to talk to the receptionist was merely a convention- al courtesy. A guy who was that worried about personal security would have had a security desk, right inside the entrance to the building. Simpson could certainly afford it.

But the thing bothering me most, the thing I

kept coming back to was that Walter had known about my date with Christine.

There was another possibility.

Big business is highly competitive. There is money to be made in corporate espionage. When I do security and threat assessment for corporations, sometimes it includes electronic counter measures. Basically, it's looking for bugs and hidden cameras in meeting rooms or other sensitive areas, and monitoring certain people's activities. You would be surprised at what forms hidden cameras or microphones can take. Cyber security has become the primary focus for most governments and multi-national corporations, even smaller business need it because the valuable data is digital. They want to protect their digital records from computer hackers or employee theft. There is any number of highly sophisticated ways to steal data. It always comes back to people though, people using electronics to get what they want.

Which is why, I can find a bug.

I went into my storage room and retrieved one of my RF, VLF, UHF and infrared scanners. Back in my office, I searched the whole room, but only found one little bug. It was a little smaller and thinner than a pack of cigarettes or a deck of cards. The microphone itself was tiny. It was attached to a battery pack that could provide power for up to 220 hours. It was stuck under the bottom of the chair at the front of my desk. It wasn't a recorder; it was a voice activated transmitter.

That was why Walter had come to my office.

He wanted to play spy.

He hadn't sent in a real professional to secure several more sophisticated devices, while I was somewhere else. He had planted this one, all by himself, with me sitting right in front of him.

Now I knew why he hadn't gone to another agency.

Walter had to have either a signal amplifier nearby, or someone parked nearby to listen in, or more likely, a receiver attached to a digital recorder. It would make it easy for someone to retrieve the recording from outside my office, at their convenience. It couldn't be far from my office though. The wireless signal range on his transmitter was only about 50 yards.

Was this the real reason Christine was coming here, to retrieve a recording?

I ruled that out when Christine showed up.

If Christine was acting, she was good at it. Her eyes were red, as if she had been crying. Her eye makeup was even smeared. She appeared to be very upset.

Why had she called me? Didn't she have a girl-friend she could call?

"Thank you for seeing me, John. I know you have better things to do than listen to me whine about my job, my former job, I should say. What a horrible day!"

"Have you called a friend or family member yet?"

She nodded. "Yes, I called my mom. She told me I had done the right thing. I guess so, but it won't be easy to find another job. She suggested I should file sexual harassment charges against Walter and Simpson Oil and Gas."

"You certainly can." I agreed.

"I'm not going to go through all of that. It would take months, and there are no witnesses on my side. I almost wish I hadn't quit, but then I remember Walter, and the goons."

She made a disgusted face.

"That sounds like a name for a 60's rock band,

'Walter and the Goons," I said.

She laughed at that.

"Today might not be as bad as you think, Christine. It just so happens, I need a receptionist and general office hand. I can't pay you as much as Simpson Oil and Gas was probably paying you, but it would help you out, till something better comes along."

She made a face I couldn't quite interpret.

"Thank you, John. That's very sweet. I know you're just trying to be helpful. I'll be alright though. It only seems terrible, right now."

The phone on my desk rang.

I looked at Christine and raised my eyebrows, to see whether I should take the call.

She nodded her response.

"Tucker Investigations, John speaking,"

It was another case of finding missing heirs for a local attorney. I got all the details and promised to investigate.

Christine had been paying close attention to my conversation.

"John, do you answer all your calls yourself?"

"Yes, even if I'm not here in the office, call forwarding goes to this cell phone. I tapped my jacket pocket. If I miss a call, they can leave a message."

"How many calls do you get in an average day?"

"I don't know, maybe a dozen."

"Do you meet with people here in the office?"

"Sure."

"How often, I mean, do you meet with clients every day?"

"Yes, nearly every day, sometimes two or three a day."

"How do you get anything done? When do you have time to do your work?" she asked.

"I told you I needed help."

"If you're serious, I'll help out, for a while."

I'm completely serious; I don't really have a new

employee handbook or anything though." I smiled

She smiled back. "We'll work out the details as we go along. One thing though…"

"What's that?"

"This office is far too small, too crowded, and pretty much too ugly."

"Oh, really?"

"We can do better, John. You need something much more professional and attractive."

"I think I have that."

"You must be kidding, this is drab and… hideous." She said.

"Oh, I agree, but things are changing. I just acquired something very professional and attractive."

She looked around the room.

"What would that be?" she asked.

"That, Christine, would be… you,"

"John, I can't work for you if you're going to hit on me, too." She frowned.

I held up my hands.

"No, no. I'm serious about how much you can help improve things around here. You're the best qualified person I could possibly have hoped for."

She smiled as she said, "Time will tell."

CHAPTER 9

I'd done more than my five thousand dollars' worth of work for Ted Simpson. I endured about ninety five million dollars' worth of annoyance. Walter Farley was on my list of least favorite people.

I decided to call Mr. Simpson directly.

"Simpson here," he answered, on the second ring.

"This is John Wesley Tucker, Mr. Simpson. I need to meet with you to discuss something that's come up."

"It better be damned important. Did Walter tell you to call me?"

"Yes sir, it is important, and no, Walter doesn't know I'm calling."

I could hear the wheels in his head grinding.

"Alright, can you come by my office at the end of business today?"

"Yes, sir, I'll be there about five o'clock."

"Fine." He hung up.

Tony ran a list of every late model Chevrolet Impala, registered to owners here in East Texas. It was far too many cars. Even allowing for the parameters we'd set, there were just too many to follow up on. We were only looking for blue cars. There were thirty-seven, late model, blue Impalas, registered in just the few counties closest to Tyler. We knew the owner of the vehicle might not be the same person as the driver we were looking for, so we couldn't really eliminate anyone. We couldn't ask the police and sheriff's departments in all those counties to investigate the owners, and any possible drivers of every blue Impala, without probable cause.

Tony ran all thirty-seven owner names through the various criminal data bases. He got several hits. There were five out of the thirty-seven, in three different counties, with arrest or criminal records. One of them had been interviewed and released already. There simply wasn't any probable cause to justify a detention and questioning of any of the rest of them.

I happened to look to my left, as I was approaching the parking lot where I'd met Dustin. Was that him in the shadows between the wall and the end of the strip mall? I couldn't turn left because of the median. I had to go all the way up to the next light, and do a U-turn.

As I pulled into the parking lot, I spotted Dustin. I hit the speed dial on my cell phone, but Tony didn't answer. I left him a quick message, as I parked in front of the strip mall, just a dozen feet from the corner of the building.

Dustin was smiling again as I approached him.

"You that angel, Good Angel," he said.

"Hello, Dustin. How are you?"

"You know how I is. I done told you."

I was confused

He grinned, then he did his little shoulder roll dance move. He ended with a laugh.

I laughed too. He had gotten me.

He looked serious.

"You ain't done. He ain't gone. The war goes on."

I nodded.

"Yes, Dustin, I know. I need your help."

He shook his head.

"Nah, suh, it's not my war."

I needed to be careful with my questions. I didn't want to lose him. I was hoping that Tony would get my message and show up quickly.

"We're looking for the car with the reindeer flying over the football."

He nodded a silent answer.

"You said it was like the sky, right?"

He nodded again.

"We're looking for a blue car with a reindeer flying over a football."

"You stupid for a angel," he snorted.

What did that mean?

"Are you saying the car isn't blue?"

"The sky ain't light in the dark of the night." He indicated.

He looked me in the eye.

"Dustin, are you saying the car is black?"

He chuckled.

"Look at me. You think I'm black? That car is darker than the belly of a cypress swamp at midnight.

"Are you sure?"

He nodded. "Oh yeah, Mister Angel, I sees it from time to time. It was the bad angel done it, he that took her."

"Have you seen it again?"

"I done told you, I sees it, from time to time."

He started to sort of rock back and forth.

I noticed a plain white car pulling into the parking lot.

Dustin saw it too.

"Who dat?" he asked.

"He's a friend of mine, Dustin. His name is Tony.

He's your friend too."

Tony got out of his car and walked over to us.

"Dustin, this is Tony."

"Uh huh, 'Tony Baloney', you messed up warrior"

What did that mean?

Tony looked at me, clearly puzzled.

Dustin nodded, he was still rocking. He pointed at the sky.

"He say you be wounded and hurtin' bad." He indicated Tony.

Tony shot me an angry look.

I needed to get this back on track.

"Tony, Dustin told me the car we're looking for isn't blue."

"Yeah, what color is it, purple?" he asked, facetiously.

Tony was clearly angry.

Dustin laughed. He was still rocking. He closed his eyes.

"They ain't watching. Folks say they do, but they ain't. Ain't nobody, got no time for that. They's singing and laughing and dancing. A lifetime here ain't but a minute there."

What was he talking about, now?

"So much joy, no sorrow there, so much joy, ain't got no care."

I had been worried about losing Dustin, but now he had completely lost me. I looked at Tony.

He was scowling, as he directed a question at Dustin.

"Dustin, did you see the man who took the little girl?"

Dustin stopped rocking, and frowned.

"They say evil ain't got no face. But the bad angel do."

"What does he look like?" I asked.

Dustin looked back and forth between me and Tony.

"He look like me, he look like you."

Tony had had enough. He turned and headed toward his unmarked Crown Victoria sedan.

"They is beautiful, you see um soon." Dustin called after Tony.

Tony got in his car and started it up.

I had to ask.

"Dustin, who is beautiful?"

He nodded at the plain white car leaving the parking lot.

"That wounded warrior's wife and boy…"

I couldn't get anything useful out of Dustin. He was our only witness and most of the time, he seemed witless. He talked nonsense and riddles. We would never be able to use him as a witness in a trial. I was discouraged. Too much time had gone by. It looked pretty hopeless.

Dustin looked at me intently.

"Keep on keepin' on, Good Angel. You is winning. I got me one more word."

"Yeah, what's that?"

"I tell you next time. I got to get to gittin'. I got my rounds."

CHAPTER 10

What had I been thinking? I arrived on the downtown square at 5.00 pm. This was one of the worst times of day to be driving into downtown Tyler, right up there with lunch-time. It was our version of rush hour and happy hour, joyfully combined in unholy matrimony. The restaurants on the square are mostly glorified bars. They appeal to young professionals, looking to hang out with peers, enjoy loud music, eat and drink, and try to hook up. There was not one open parking place on the square, or within two blocks of it.

I ended up parking in the same place I had before, hoping I hadn't accidently joined the Church of England. By the time I rode the elevator up to the top floor of the Simpson building, it was nearly 5:20.

Today, there was no beautiful receptionist to greet me. She was working for me now.

Instead, there was a young, burly guy, with a crew cut, wearing an off the rack suit that didn't really fit him. He must have weighed in at 275. He looked like he could bench-press twice that. Simpson had visible security now.

I smiled my warmest smile.

"Hello, I'm John Wesley Tucker. I have an appointment with Mr. Simpson."

The security guy kind of smirked. It might have been a gas pain.

He pushed a button on the intercom.

Christine had walked down the hall to Mr. Simpson's office. I remembered that quite clearly.

"There's somebody here to see you, Mr. Simpson, says his name is Tucker."

"Send him in." Mr. Simpson replied.

The security guy inclined his head down the hall. He was working as a security guard, but he wasn't worth the price of his clip-on tie. He let me carry a gun into a meeting with his boss.

"Tucker, you're late," Mr. Simpson said, by way of greeting.

"Yes, sir. I apologize. If this is not a good time for you, I'll make another appointment."

"We'll talk now. What do you want, more money?" He glared at me.

"No, sir. I wanted to tell you I am finished working for you."

"You could have just given your report to Walter. You're wasting my time." He said.

"That's what I wanted to talk to you about. I have not completed my investigation. I have found things of concern, but I expect you know all about it."

He narrowed his eyes at me.

"What kind of things?"

"I'm sure Walter has kept you informed. He's the reason I'm quitting. I no longer wish to work for you."

"What the hell are you talking about?" He pushed a button on his intercom. "Walter, get in here."

I decided to get straight to the point.

"Walter has bugged my office." I informed him.

"... He did what?"

Walter strolled in.

"Ah, Mr. Tucker, what an unexpected surprise, I believe I instructed you not to bother Mr. Simpson." He said smugly.

"Can it, Walter. What's this about you bugging Mr. Tucker's office?"

Walter paled slightly.

"I don't think I know what…"

"Damn it, Walter, cut the crap. Did you bug his office or not?"

Walter looked down at the carpet.

"Mr. Tucker has been uncooperative and refuses to be forthcoming with the results of his investigation. I was merely trying to ensure a steady and reliable flow of information."

Mr. Simpson took a deep breath and blew it out slowly.

"OK. You may go now, Walter. I want to talk to Mr. Tucker, alone."

Walter gave me a vacant look as he left the office, carefully closing the door on his way out.

Mr. Simpson fixed his attention on me. "Listen, Tucker, I apologize for what he did. I had no idea Walter would do something like that. He is intensely loyal to me, a trait I value above all others. He was just trying to be clever."

"Whatever. The point is I'm done. You can find another agency to do your investigating."

"Yeah, I can see how you would be damned mad about what he did. I don't blame you for wanting to quit. What if I offer you more money?"

I shook my head.

"Well then, at least tell me what you've learned, so far. I paid you to do some work for me, and you're standing in my office. What have you got?"

"What has Walter told you?"

"… Nothing. The topic hasn't come up, until all this mess."

I told him everything I had told Walter, and brought him up to speed on where I was at this point in the investigation.

"… I was about to talk to your wife," I concluded.

Mr. Simpson was still sitting in his massive desk chair, leaned back with his finger-tips together, and his feet up on the desk.

"You are very thorough, aren't you? I'm not currently planning to run for national office, just state office. You took hold of the bull by the nose, boy. I think you've done quite enough. I'd like to have you on the payroll. Would you consider working for me as my head of security? I'd make it worth your while."

I actually considered it, for about half a second.

"No sir. I'm pretty content doing what I'm doing. I worked for Uncle Sam for just a little too long. I'm happy being self-employed."

He was silent for a moment. Then he opened his jacket and took out his check book.

"You know, people don't usually say 'no' to me." He observed.

He finished writing out the check. He stood up and came around his desk. I stood up as well. The meeting was clearly over.

"What Walter did was wrong. He could have jeopardized your business. He violated our trust. That bothers me most. I hope this little bonus will help you think better of me, and maybe we can do business together again some time."

He handed me the check. I accepted it and put it in my jacket pocket.

We shook hands.

I didn't look at the check, until I was riding the elevator down to the lobby.

It was for twenty five thousand dollars.

I was definitely going to deposit this one.

It was dusk, by the time I walked out of the Simpson building. I hit the sidewalk and headed back to where my car was parked, three blocks away. I knew I was being followed. At first, I had just sensed something was wrong.

It started with a vague uneasy feeling, as soon as I left the Simpson building. A lot of things can make a person feel uneasy; maybe a simple concern, like whether or not you remembered to lock up when you left your car. Maybe it's some sort of guilty feeling about something you should have done, or said, or something you shouldn't have. Maybe you're starting to get a cold or the flu. Sometimes, it's just something you ate.

Survival instinct is different. When you've spent your whole life learning how to survive in a dangerous world, on a hostile planet, you begin to develop survival instinct. Over time, you fine-tune it.

That's why I was able to spot the man tailing me. Because I was fully alert, I sensed him before I saw him. At first, when I looked on the other side of the street, there was a small flock of people on the square, and nothing appeared menacing. Scanning the flock, I saw nothing out of the ordinary. Turning a corner thinned the flock. I noticed one man leave the flock. He was headed in the same direction as me, pretty much matching my pace.

I normally walk just a little faster than the average person. I always have. I walk a little faster, because I'm never just strolling. I'm on my way somewhere specific, and a steady pace gets me there more quickly. I'm basically wired to move. Consequently, someone matching my pace, to keep up, is obvious to me. In this war, just as a predator can quickly identify its prey, I can spot a predator.

This guy appeared to be pretty ordinary. He was white, a little taller than me, and a little heavier maybe. His hair was cut short and might have been brown. He wore a tan windbreaker-type jacket half zipped, over some sort of black polo style shirt, with dark green pants.

I turned into an alley, fully aware I might be trapped in there. I heard him pick up his pace, the moment he saw me turn into the alley.

I was ready for him when he followed me in. As he came around the corner, I was waiting to meet him. I had my Browning Hi Power in my hand, just in case.

Good thing too.

He had unzipped his jacket and produced a Glock, with a silencer on it. He came into the alley prepared to fire. I realized he was there to kill me, at about the same time he realized I wasn't where he had expected to see me. We were only about twenty feet apart.

We both fired at about the same time.

His Glock spit three quick, sound-suppressed shots, in the time it took me to fire my first one. All three of his shots struck the dumpster I was hiding behind, and careened by, within an inch of my face. I felt them go by - hot, whistling 9mm lead.

My first and second shots hit him center mass, and staggered him. I thought one bullet might have hit his firing arm, because he never re-acquired me as a target. My third bullet went through his throat, just below his chin. He fell like a rag doll.

The sound of my Browning firing in the confines of that alley had been deafening. As I stood and walked over to him, my ears were ringing. He was dead when I reached him.

My first two bullets had only staggered him, because under his black polo shirt, he was wearing black Kevlar body armor. When I rolled him over to complete my search for I.D., his head twisted loosely. Apparently my 9mm round had severed his spine at the base of his skull, leaving a gory exit wound. There wasn't much blood because his heart had been stopped instantly.

He had no I.D. Other than a Timex wristwatch, he had no jewelry either. He had no immediately visible tattoos or other markings. He was a pro.

He was a pro, as in "had-been." Now he was nothing but a couple of hundred pounds of bio-matter, to be cleaned up and buried. The man was no longer here. He had gone on to judgment.

My hands began shaking, and I felt weak in the knees. I staggered over to the dumpster and worked on catching my breath. After a few moments, I called it in. I stayed on the phone with my friend, Detective Tony Escalante, even as I heard the sirens approaching. Obviously, I hadn't been the first person to call. There were a lot of people around the square, and as loud as the gunfire had sounded to me, they probably heard it all over town. The 911 operators had suddenly found themselves very busy.

CHAPTER 11

The first cops on the scene took my Browning, cuffed me, and stuffed me in the back seat of a patrol car. That's where Tony Escalante found me. He was the first detective on the scene. He looked at me in the patrol car, then walked away and started talking to one of the patrol officers. They had the whole area cordoned off with crime scene tape.

It was dusk, and the light was fading in the alley. Portable lights soon lit the area as bright as day. By now, the local news vans were there, filming everything. There were half a dozen uniforms doing crowd control, talking on their radios, and waiting for the paramedics to leave.

The crime scene techs showed up and began photographing everything in situ. From the backseat of the patrol car, I could see them placing little placards with numbers on the filthy and poorly maintained surface of the alley, marking the locations of the spent shell casings.

Tony carefully studied the scene and knelt down examining the body. He spent some time conversing with one of the uniforms who held some rank. Eventually, he sent a patrolman over to the car. I was expecting to be let out of the back seat, but the patrolman drove me to the station and stuck me in a holding cell.

I sat alone in a cell for about two hours before I was taken to an interview room and cuffed to the table. I figured it had probably been at least three hours since the shooting, maybe more.

After a while, Tony came in to do the interview. He was carrying a file folder. He dropped it on the table top, but he didn't sit down. He crossed his arms and nodded at me.

"This interview is being recorded. I'm Detective Anthony Escalante. We have your name as being John Wesley Tucker. Is that correct?"

"Hello, Tony, it's nice to see you, too."

"This is an official investigation into a fatal shooting which occurred earlier this evening. If you would prefer it, Mr. Tucker, I can have another detective do the interview. Hell, maybe I should just read you your rights and throw you back into a cell, instead."

"Well, as you can see, I'm already in custody. So, if I'm actually under arrest, you have to read me my rights, or take these cuffs off and let me go."

Apparently he did not find my comment, tone, or attitude amusing. I figured he should at least be amused to see me cuffed to the table.

"Tell me what happened in the alley, Mr. Tucker.",

I could've held out for my rights and demanded an attorney, forcing his hand. I could've sat silently, refusing to cooperate, frustrating him in his efforts to learn exactly what had happened. I was tempted to do the latter, just to watch him get angry. I didn't do any of those things, because I appreciated Tony's position and I knew nothing I said would be admissible in court.

"OK, Detective Escalante, here's the way it went down..." I told him the story.

"… I ducked down behind a dumpster the second I went into the alley. He was good. He came in there to kill me, and he nearly did. He fired three shots. I think he tried to hit me in the head with all three. My eyes and my gun arm were the only parts exposed from behind the dumpster, and he spotted me instantly. He was good." I said again.

"Did you know him, the man who shot at you?"

"I have no idea who he was. I checked him for ID, but he was clean."

"Mr. Tucker, do you know why he was trying to kill you?"

I raised my eyebrows and looked up at Tony.

The corners of his mouth twitched a little.

"Yeah, you do have a tendency to piss people off." he nodded. Then he remembered himself. "Answer the question, Mr. Tucker." He instructed me.

"No, Detective Escalante, I'd never seen him before in my life."

He was thoughtful for a while. I waited to see where this was going. It appeared for a moment as if Tony had completed the interview. Then he spoke up.

"Ok. Here's what we know, so far. Your story checks out, as near as we can tell from evidence at the scene. We found his 9mm shell casings and yours. We traced the shots fired from his Glock to the dumpster where they glanced off. The position of your shell casings supports your being crouched behind the dumpster. He had on Kevlar body armor, which saved his life from your double tap. He had a sound suppressor on his Glock, not the sort of thing we see much of…"

"… Yeah, and he knew how to use that weapon. He fired three shots very fast, and he barely missed me," I interrupted.

Tony nodded.

"We recovered two of the bullets you fired at him, from the Kevlar. You were very lucky with the third shot…"

I shrugged, and interrupted again "… Actually, I was aiming for his head."

Tony gave me a dirty look.

"He had no identification, just like you said. We ran his prints and the only thing we came up with is his military service record. Army, spec ops, he was a Sergeant and a squad leader. Saw action in two tours in Afghanistan. Further investigation brought up some personal info. He left with an honorable discharge and apparently went to work as a hired gun. He's been questioned by the FBI on a couple of occasions, but has no arrest record. He's never been charged with anything, but he was a suspected button man, and probably would do gun work for anybody who paid him."

He regarded me again, still with some animosity.

"Mr. Tucker, do you have any idea who might have sent him after you?"

"No, Detective Escalante, nothing I can be sure of."

"… Theories?"

"No, Detective Escalante, I've got nothing."

"… And you're sure you never met him?"

I nodded.

"Answer the question."

Oh yeah, for the microphone.

"No, Detective Escalante, I never saw the man before today when he followed me into the alley, and I have no idea why he was trying to kill me."

Tony was thoughtful again for a moment.

"Very well, there are no charges being filed against you, at this time. You're free to go."

"I'd like my gun back."

"… Eventually. We'll hold onto your Browning for now. Your other personal property is at the front desk. You can get it on the way out." He simply walked out, leaving me cuffed to the table.

A few minutes later, a uniformed officer came and released me. He took me to the front desk where I got my jacket, tie, shoes, belt, wallet, watch, pocket knife, empty holster, car keys and self-respect back. The check was still in the jacket pocket.

At 9:30, I was sitting in the bar at the Olive Garden, when Tony came in. Technically, his shift had ended at 8:00, but he had caught my case, and had to finish the paper work. Like every day for the last few months, Tony came here to eat, drink, and remember. He sat in the bar, because it was right in the middle of the restaurant, well-lit and public. It helped him regulate his drinking.

In practice they closed the place at 10:00, but several employees didn't get to go home till midnight. The manager was a friend of Tony's. He knew what I knew.

Tony didn't want to go home to an empty house, and find himself alone, drinking, with his service gun in his hand.

This restaurant was one of Marcia's favorites.

Tony's wife, Marcia, and son, Billy, had been in the ground for three months. Ninety days of grief turned to depression. Today was the anniversary of the day Tony had lost them to the highway. Tony's wife had drifted off the shoulder at 70 miles per hour, on I-20, headed toward Dallas. She over-corrected, veered suddenly across the highway, hit the median, and rolled the SUV. They were both pronounced dead at the scene.

I had a cold beer waiting for him.

"Hey Tony"

"J.W." he nodded. "Don't you get tired of coming here all the time? I think I see you here two or three times a week."

It had taken me a few weeks to figure out what he was doing with most of his evenings. I had only met him here, maybe a dozen times over the last few months. I was keeping an eye on him.

He was just now figuring it out.

"I will, when you do," I replied.

"You OK?" he asked.

"Terrific, considering the way the day ended."

"You're lucky we live in Texas. If this had been California or New York, you would still be in a jail cell, having been charged with manslaughter.

"Oh come on, Tony. I'm a licensed professional and I have a concealed carry permit. In America, a man has a right to defend himself when he's attacked."

"In this part of America, maybe, other parts of America, not so much."

"Who was that guy?"

"His name was Hudson, Jefferson Hudson. He went by 'Huddy' back in his uniform days. He was a real bad boy, J.W. You're lucky to be alive."

"I don't believe in luck."

"Yeah, I know. The point is somebody wants you dead. They hired a hitter. He didn't even try to make it look like an accident. I don't expect they'll stop, till they stop you. Who have you crossed this time?"

I considered the implications of his statement.

"I really don't know who or why, at this point. I'm working a couple of cases that could go sideways. Sometimes it's something from the past. I just don't know."

"Officially, I can't offer you any help. You know you can count on me, personally and un-officially."

"I know, Tony, thanks."

"Guys like him might not even know who they work for. There could be several layers of cutouts." Tony reminded me.

"I know that too."

He nodded, and sipped at his beer. I noticed his hand begin to shake. He set down the glass and gripped it very tightly, so tightly, I was afraid he would break it.

"I wish it had been me in the alley. I wish the guy had shot and killed me." He said it quietly, but with intense conviction.

"No, Tony. No you don't. I know you're struggling, but you've got to hold on."

"Why?" he choked. "Why would God... do this, to me?"

Good question. I had nothing to say. I can't answer for God. Should I tell Tony everything was going to be alright? Should I point out the fact God is God and not answerable to our limited understanding of His plans and purposes? Should I mention being angry at God is sort of foolish?

He composed himself.

"I do take some comfort from knowing they're in heaven. I know I will see them again," he sighed.

I nodded.

"The thing is this, how do I go on without them? Where do I go from here?" He asked.

I waited a beat.

"Do you mean after you leave the Olive Garden? I hear IHOP is nice, and they're always open."

His head snapped around.

I lifted my eyebrows, innocently.

He laughed. He hadn't laughed in a long time.

"We're both alive, Tony. We have to go on; we just keep putting one foot in front of the other, till the race is run."

He sighed and nodded.

"Yeah, I know. So what's your next move?"

"Tomorrow is another day. My next move is to get some sleep. I'll see you, Tony."

"Be careful."

"Right back at you," I gave a little wave on my way out.

CHAPTER 12

I saw Dustin again the next morning on my way to my office. He was pushing his cart down the sidewalk on the east side of south Broadway. He was headed south toward the park that runs along the edge of the creek. I pulled into the parking lot of a big hotel and walked down to the trail beside the creek. After a couple of minutes, Dustin came along pushing his cart.

He grinned when he saw me.

"Hello, Good Angel. I got a word for you." He said seriously. "I know its name."

Was he referring to the "bad angel"?

"Hello, Dustin. How are you?"

He raised his eyebrows at me.

Oh yeah, I remembered, "he done told me".

"What name is that?"

He handed me his bible.

"It's written in the Word," he said.

Uh oh. There is a lot written in the Word.

He saw the look on my face, and laughed. "You got to open it to read it. You stupid - for a good angel."

His bible was full of all sorts of page markers. He had leaves, feathers, scraps of paper, bits of string, even a ten dollar bill, stuck here and there, all through it. I didn't have a clue where to start.

My phone rang. It was Christine, so I answered it.

"I'm waiting in the parking lot. Are you coming to open the office?"

"Yes, sorry, I'm on my way." I hung up.

Dustin was studying me.

"Dustin, I'm sorry, I have to go. I don't have time to read everything in your bible."

"Then you gots to read this," he said. He pulled a scrap of paper out of his bible and handed it to me. I looked at it. The only thing written on it was GEN 416.

Was this a reference to Genesis, chapter four and verse sixteen?

I looked at Dustin.

He smiled and nodded.

"Word," he said, and he walked away, pushing his cart.

When I parked at the office, Christine was standing under the green and white striped awning at the entrance. Today, she was wearing a teal colored t-shirt with fancy embroidery on the front. The t-shirt was tucked into her tan jeans and she had a belt festooned with sparkling crystals. Her teal colored tennis shoes had embroidery on them as well. Her flaming red hair blazed in the sunlight, with copper and golden highlights. As usual, she wore it loose and unadorned. She smiled when she saw me approaching.

"I'm sorry if I rushed you," she said. "I just wanted to make sure you were coming to open the office. I'll bet there are days when you don't come to the office at all."

"No problem, Christine. You're right, I do keep uneven hours. It will be a huge help having you here, when I can't come in."

I unlocked the office and handed Christine the extra key.

"I know we're looking for a bigger office, but until we find it, you'll need a key. This one is yours."

Our office was kind of embarrassing to behold. Christine's desk was a folding plastic table from Walmart. Her chair was a folding plastic chair from the same store. The office was now very crowded. I was actually looking forward to moving.

I pulled out the scrap of paper that Dustin had given me. I looked up Genesis 4:16. It said that Cain had taken up residence in the land of Nod, east of Edom.

What did that mean? Was the kidnapper a man named Cain, or maybe, Nod?

There is a town called Edom, a few miles west of Tyler.

But the passage said east of Edom. There are many towns that are east of Edom; including Tyler, and every other city between here and the eastern seaboard.

I looked up Genesis 41:6. It said that seven heads of grain appeared, and were withered by the east wind.

Huh? Oh please! No help there, either.

I didn't get it, not at all. I was worried that I had put too much confidence in Dustin.

I called Tony to ask if he could shoot with me that evening. He agreed, but he sounded annoyed and made it a 'maybe, if' instead of a definite "yes."

I called Gary Babcock to get him started on the new insurance fraud case. Gary is one of my part time operatives. He's a fireman by profession, but because of his shift schedule, he has a lot of days and nights to work a second job. I use him for surveillance and photography. He's a big guy that fits in nicely in any situation which doesn't require white collar sophistication. He can pass for any kind of utility serviceman, exterminator or construction worker. He's quite comfortable in truck stops, barbecue joints and sports bars. He blends in because he is such an ordinary looking guy. He's content to sit in a car and wait, watching a subject. He has also proven to be a good enough actor, to put insurance fraud suspects into situations that test their claims of injury.

Once, while posing as a new neighbor, he invited one insurance fraud suspect to go hunting with him. When the opportunity to take a twelve point buck was offered, the guy was miraculously healed. Using a camouflage game camera, we got him on film, scurrying up a ladder and setting up a tree stand. The insurance company put his head up on their wall.

I wasn't bothered with the ringing telephone, because Christine answered every incoming call, and I was impressed at her ability to do "triage," setting appointments for people whose need was not urgent, taking messages and only putting me on the phone with the people I really needed to talk to. She employed hand-signal and facial expressions to secure my responses, while she repeated the name of the person on the line.

Later in the day, I introduced her to some of the web-sites I use for locating heirs and finding current locations for people. She started doing some simple name searches. She was a natural.

I was learning other things about Christine. She told me about her struggles with intimacy. She doesn't like to be touched by people she doesn't know well. She wants to be loved and to be in love, but she is afraid of intimacy. Her issues go back to somewhere in her development. Ever since her last boyfriend hurt her, she has been unable to allow herself to get close to any man. It's sad, because she is "all that, and a bag of chips".

Tony did meet me at the shooting range. I got there ahead of him and arranged for our usual shooting stations. When Tony walked in, I could tell he was not happy to see me.

"Hey, Tony, I talked to Dustin, again."

"Why'd you tell that homeless nutcase about my family, J.W.?" Were the first angry words out of his mouth.

"Believe me, Tony, I didn't tell him anything about you, except that you're my friend."

He scowled at me, clearly doubting my words, and maybe doubting our friendship.

"Tony, I swear, I didn't say anything to him."

"Well, how do you explain what he said to me?" he asked.

"Uh, I can't. He says things that are off the wall, mixed in with things that make sense. He told me the Impala we're looking for is black, not blue."

"… Big help that is. Tomorrow, it will probably be green or yellow."

He unzipped his gun bag.

"Well, no, I don't think so. I misunderstood him the first time he described it." I said, tentatively.

"We have nothing J.W., except the video tape from the supermarket, and the photo found in the parking lot. Everything else is based on the silly jabbering of a mentally incompetent homeless man," Tony said, as he put on his shooting glasses.

"He was right about the Impala and the location where the girl was taken."

"Maybe," Tony shrugged, pulling his hearing protectors down over his ears.

Further conversation would have to wait. I knew I needed to put on my ear protection as well. Tony was preparing to fire the big .50 caliber Desert Eagle, he had just pulled out of his gun bag.

CHAPTER 13

"... I think we should go look at it together," Christine concluded.

She'd called a real estate agency and they'd suggested an office in a high rise, right on the south loop, just a couple of blocks east of Broadway.

"Get this - it used to be an office for the ATF. Talk about security, it has bullet proof walls and windows, and places where cameras were mounted to watch the hallway approaches and the entrance. The cameras are gone, but the mounts and wiring are still in place. I'll bet you'd like that."

"I'm not as paranoid as Uncle Sam, Christine. We just need more space, not a fortress."

"Fine, but it doesn't cost any more than the other offices in the building. Prices are down right now in this economy. I think we can afford it. Come on, it might be fun."

I liked the way she had said "we" could afford it. It had been just "me" for too long.

"OK, get an appointment and we'll go look at it."

The building was ten stories tall. The first floor housed a bank, with attendant security. Two sets of elevators serviced the upper floors. The office in question was one of three on the sixth floor. The other offices on the sixth floor, housed two law firms, very upscale law firms.

Christine was right. I saw where the cameras had been mounted at the end of the hall, right outside the heavy, beautiful walnut door of the office suite that had recently housed the ATF. There was a digital card reader mounted on the door, as well as a key lock.

The stairs at this end of the building had a doorway nearby, and the restrooms were very convenient. I liked the whole set up. It was far and away better than my little space in a strip-mall about two miles away. I was pretty sure it was more than I deserved, probably more than I could afford, and I hadn't even seen the actual office space yet.

When I did see it, I was impressed. The front door opened to an oak paneled reception area, with windows at the back. There were two doors off the reception area, one on each side. The door on the right, led to a long room with windows all down the outside. The marks on the carpet, the variety of outlets and cable connections indicated there had been partitions to divide the room up into individual work stations. In the corner, there was a small area with a vinyl floor that had clearly been a break room area. There was also a door that opened out into the hallway. It would have allowed ATF employees to enter and leave the work area, without having to go through the reception area. That door had a card reader and key lock on the outside, as well.

The door on the left side of the reception area, led into a single office paneled in walnut, with built in book cases. One wall was windows. I took a moment to enjoy the view. South Tyler in particular is heavily forested. The view from up here was like looking at a park or nature preserve. I was reminded, like so many things in life; it was just a curtain, blocking off the view of other things. Under the canopy of trees, were the homes and businesses of thousands of people.

In this office, there was a door in a walnut paneled wall that led into another room nearly as large as the office. I couldn't tell what it had been used for. That room had a door out into the hallway, set up the same way as the other doors. It appeared to be useful for entering or leaving the office suite, without using the front entrance, just like on the other side. I figured all together, the suite was at least 1,750 square feet. My current office was only about the size of the reception area in this suite. I imagined properly furnishing a space this big could become very expensive, very quickly.

After we looked at the office suite, I took Christine to lunch at Chuy's.

"If you can get a six month lease for less than two grand a month, we'll take it," I said.

"Wahooo!" She exclaimed.

"Well hold on, you don't know if we can get it for those terms."

"Oh yes we can! I already got the management company to commit to twelve fifty a month, on a six month lease. They'll be thrilled to get it leased. It's been sitting empty for more than six months."

She was beaming at me.

"I can do all the decorating. I'll make it look like you are the most successful P.I. in the city. Just you wait. You'll see. This is a really good thing."

"I agree, Christine, you've convinced me. I'm kind of excited about it myself. And you won't have to worry about losers like Walter anymore."

I immediately regretted having mentioned Walter. Her face clouded up, and I felt low because I had upset her.

"Speaking of Walter, if I were you, I'd teach

him a lesson he would never forget. He could have ruined your business, not to mention the way he treated me. I can't stand to let him get away with it. Let's punish him! You know what they say about payback." She suggested.

"No, we won't."

"Why not, I know you aren't afraid of him. Are you afraid he'd send his goons?"

"No, that's not it. I don't believe in getting even. I believe because I've been forgiven, I should forgive others."

"Oh, for crying out loud! Do you just let scumbags and low-life's walk all over you?"

"No, I don't. I just don't allow myself to take revenge for offenses. I remember that I'm no better than they are, really. I have said and done things I regret. I have on occasion treated people badly. Don't get me wrong, I get mighty annoyed when people act like idiots, drive poorly, act rudely, and play their music too loud. I try to remember I've been guilty of all those things myself, at one time or another, everybody has. When people deliberately offend me, I choose not to hold on to the offense, I try to let it go, like water rolling off a duck's back. "

She considered my response for a moment.

"Well, I'd like to think I'm better than some people I know." She said.

I nodded.

"Yep, we all do. Sometimes looking down on others makes us feel better about ourselves. When we compare ourselves to others, and start feeling superior, we forget that everybody sins and falls short. No matter how good we think we are, our own righteousness is no better than dirty diapers, from God's point of view. Nobody can measure up to God's standard of righteousness. That's why He sent Jesus to pay the price. Only Jesus was perfect. Nobody else can ever be good enough. "

She shook her head.

"You religious types crack me up. People like Walter are just wicked and self-serving."

"We're all self-serving, Christine, and we all have a little streak of wickedness in us. If we start by seeing our own limitations and failings, we get along better with other people. Besides, what Walter did actually benefitted us."

"… How's that?"

"Well, you work for me now, Christine. We're getting to move into a great new space, and Walter's foolish behavior is paying for the move. Mr. Simpson felt so bad about what Walter did he gave me a bonus check. It's enough money to pay for the new office."

She grinned.

"Maybe there is a little justice in the world."

CHAPTER 14

On the way to my next appointment about fifteen miles south of Tyler, in the town of Jacksonville, I dropped Christine off at the office. I was driving south, on highway 69. Often, when I'm driving, I listen to talk radio.

"Human beings are just highly evolved apes. We have canine teeth and finger-nails, for biting and tearing. We're just smarter than the other, less evolved apes. We invented weapons to kill with, which put us at the top of the food chain. That's survival of the fittest, baby."

"Hmmph, I don't consider our animal ancestry to be a sufficient reason to eat meat. If you were a more evolved human being, like I am, you'd understand the only sensible diet for people, is vegetarian or vegan. Vegetables, legumes and other plants are a renewable food source and they don't pollute the planet. No animals are tortured and killed to provide food for me. If you think the killing of fish, birds and other animals for food, is appropriate, you're barbaric!"

To me, the debate seemed... tasteless.

Once again, I wondered why I ever listened to talk radio. It offered endless opinions, but very little useful or intelligent perspective, and no light.

As I turned the radio off, I noticed the car in front of me was a black Impala.

I speed dialed Tony's cell.

"Detective Escalante here, what can I do for you?"

"Tony, it's John, I need you to run a license plate for me."

"Apparently, J.W., you presume I'm your personal mole into the DMV data base. Wrong!"

I was startled by Tony's attitude. Evidently, he was still angry about the incident with Dustin.

"Tony, this is important. Please run this plate. We need to find out who the owner of the car is."

"Why do you want that information?"

"I'm headed south towards Jacksonville. I'm right behind a black Impala. The license plate is GEN 416. That's G as in Giraffe, E as in Elephant, N as in Nancy, four, one, six. A black Impala, Tony! I think this is the car."

"Oh yeah, is that what you think? Well, every-body has an opinion. They're as common as belly buttons. Personally, I think most stand-up comedy is really pretty disgusting."

"Come on, Tony... Dustin gave me the license number."

"Let me see if I understand you correctly. You're following a car with a license number, some crack-pot gave you, and you want me to find out who the car belongs to, that about it, wild man?"

"Tony, just consider the possibility, I could be right. Are you willing to let a child abductor go, just because you resent me asking you to check a license number? If I'm wrong, there's no harm, no foul. If I'm right, we can get this guy."

There was no answer for a moment. I was afraid he had hung up on me.

"J.W., something's come up. I'll get back to you,"

He hung up on me.

As we approached a red light, I pulled up next to the black Impala.

The driver was an ordinary-looking white guy. He had short brown hair and a goatee. He looked to be in his thirties. He was wearing a grey, hooded sweatshirt, a ball cap and sunglasses.

I followed the Impala south for ten minutes. When Tony called me back, we were on the overpass, at the town of Bullard.

"Are you still behind the Impala?" he asked.

"Yep, we just went through Bullard."

"Can you keep an eye on it, for a while longer?"

There was tension in his voice.

"Sure, Tony, in this traffic, we're all headed south, I can keep him in sight. Why?"

"There are several things happening. I ran the plate. The guy who owns the Impala lives here in Tyler. He has a record, J.W. I don't have probable cause, or even enough information to get a warrant to search his apartment, but I'm sending a patrol car over there, just to take a look around, and maybe interview some of his neighbors."

He was stressed. I could hear it in his voice.

"Tony, what's going on? This is the guy, isn't it?"

Tony sighed.

"I'm headed south, toward you, right now. I want to know where he is, and where he's going. We don't have any probable cause to stop him, J.W."

That was the problem. Tony knew we were looking at the right guy, but there was no legal reason to interfere with him.

"What do you want me to do?"

"Just don't lose him. I've alerted DPS. They're sending a unit your way. We'll figure something out."

I saw the Impala's left turn signal go on. I put mine on as well

"Tony, he's leaving the highway. He's heading east on a little county road, near Mt. Selman. I'll tell you the number in a minute."

"Don't lose him." Tony snapped.

"Calm down. You know where he lives. You can pick him up any time you want. What's the big deal about keeping him in sight?"

Tony was silent for a moment.

"J.W., there's another little girl missing. She was taken about forty minutes ago. There is no actual connection to this guy or his car, but I need to know where he goes. It could be important. I'm just approaching Bullard, now. What's that county road?"

I told him, my mind racing.

"What if I cause a wreck? I could hit him with my car. Maybe I could disable his vehicle, and we might get a look in his trunk."

We had entered a heavily-wooded and very hilly area. The road curved up and down, through heavy pine and mixed hardwood forest.

"Don't do that, J.W., something could go very wrong. If the little girl is in the trunk, she could be hurt or killed. Don't spook him and try not to lose him."

I had a hard time understanding him, because the cell phone signal was breaking up.

"Yeah, but easier said than done. He has to know I'm behind him. We're the only two cars headed out here, in the deep-woods. Hang on, he's leaving the road. I'll have to go on past him."

The driver of the Impala had stopped at a pipe gate, the entrance to a private gravel road, disappearing back into the forest. As I drove by, he got out of the Impala and went to unlock the gate. In my rear-view mirror, I saw him open the gate, but then I went around a curve, and the forest blocked my view. I tried to relay the information to Tony, but the cell phone signal was breaking up. I had no bars on my phone. I had to drive nearly a mile before I could find a safe place to turn around. I now had no cell-phone signal, at all.

When I got back to the pipe gate, it was closed and the Impala was out of sight. I got out of my car and checked the gate. It was locked with a padlock.

I ducked under the single joint of welded pipe, which made up the gate, working my way into the forest, along the edge of the gravel road. The gravel gave out after about twenty yards, the road becoming just two dirt tracks, twisting through the mixed timber. The underbrush along the edge of the road was mostly blackberry thickets, brambles and coarse bushes. It was too tangled and close for me to creep through the woods in my sport coat.

I went back to my car to gear up.

Tony drove up a moment later. He saw what I was getting ready to do.

"J.W. we can't go in there. It would be trespassing on private property. I'm a cop from Tyler. I can't… I don't have any jurisdiction out here. I'm not even sure what county we're in."

"Well, I think we're probably in Cherokee County, and if you don't have any jurisdiction, then you can't stop me from going in there."

Tony was troubled. I could see he was trying to figure out some legal way to handle the situation.

I ducked under the gate.

"Hold on a minute. I'm coming with you," he said.

He went to the back of the unmarked Tyler police car and opened the trunk. I couldn't see what he was doing. When he closed the trunk, he was wearing a bullet-proof vest, under a light jacket, with 'POLICE' stenciled on it. He was carrying a twelve gauge, pump action shotgun.

Now we were ready.

CHAPTER 15

We walked up the dirt road, side by side, speaking quietly.

Tony told me the man we were after was named Evan Whitaker. He had a conviction for molestation and was a registered sex offender. He had been questioned and released, the day after Victoria was taken.

"I only got far enough in here to see there's a building up ahead. You can see the fresh car tracks where the Impala came in."

"If we see anything suspicious, we'll go back to the car and radio for backup," Tony said.

When we got to the spot where I had stopped before, we could both see the outline of a building, just around a curve in the road, broken up by the trees and brush.

We eased our way as best we could through the thickets of brush and brambles into the mixed timber forest. We went into the woods because we wanted the cover, and to make our approach to the building from a different direction than the road in.

As we got closer, we could see the building was

an older, single-wide mobile home, sitting in a clearing. The Impala was parked right in front of the little porch outside the front door. The trunk was open.

We stopped to discuss our options.

"Now we know all we need to know. Let's go back out to the road and do some planning. We'll coordinate with the Cherokee County Sheriff's office. We can set up surveillance on this place and his apartment. If we see anything suspicious, we'll pick him up for questioning."

"No, Tony, we need to go ahead and arrest him, right now."

"... On what charge? We don't have any evidence against him."

"Yes we do. We have a witness who saw him hit Victoria Winslow and put her into the trunk of that car. Dustin even gave us the license plate."

"Yeah? Some nutty homeless guy, who won't be able to testify in court."

"Tony, stop thinking about Dustin's disability and focus on the facts."

I could see Tony trying to think of a response.

"It's too dangerous. If he sees us coming, he can escape out the back, or open fire on us from inside the trailer." He pointed out.

"What if those kids are in there? Can you leave them there with him? I can't. I'm going to go have a look in the trunk of that Impala."

Tony tried to stop me, but I ducked past him, and ran in a crouch to the side of the Impala. At any moment, the man inside the mobile home could come out to close the trunk, and find me crouched beside it. I had half expected the suspect to open the front door and shoot me on sight.

Staying hidden behind the car, I took a quick look into the trunk.

There was nothing in the trunk, except a roll of duct tape and a small, pink tennis shoe.

I looked across at Tony and nodded my head, pointing at the trunk.

Tony sprinted across and crouched down next to me. He took a quick look into the trunk.

"How do you want to handle this?" I asked him.

"I need to get some back up in here, fast." Tony pulled out his cell phone.

From inside the mobile home, we heard a little girl scream.

"No signal here, Tony. It's time to go in. There are only two doors into that mobile home, the front and the back, which one do you want?"

"Are you trying to get us killed?" He asked me.

"Do you plan to live forever?"

Tony looked down at the ground for a moment. When he looked back up, he was grim.

"I'll take the front door, you take the back," he said.

Tony told me he would give me sixty seconds to get to the back door, and then he would just walk up onto the porch and knock on the door. He would get the drop on Whitaker when he opened the door. I was just supposed to prevent him from bolting out the back door.

Less than a minute later, I was on the back porch with my .45 in my hand. When I heard Tony's knock on the front door, I tried the back door handle, very gently. It wasn't locked.

I couldn't see anything inside the trailer, but I heard someone slam a door closed somewhere inside. I could hear a little girl crying, and I could sense movement toward the front door.

I opened the back door and stepped into a laundry room. Just as I reached the door into the hallway, I heard the sound of a shotgun being racked, off to my left. The boom of that shotgun being fired was like an explosion. The shot had come from inside the trailer. I raced into the living area and saw Whitaker throw open the front door. The cheap exterior door had a massive hole in it. I knew he had shot Tony through the door without even opening it. He racked his shotgun to fire again. I yelled.

"Whitaker, drop it."

He was in the process of aiming his shotgun, but he froze and looked back over his shoulder at me.

He was looking into the barrel of my .45, from less than ten feet away. I wouldn't miss.

I saw him process the fact he couldn't hope to swing his long gun around toward me, without me blowing a hole through is head.

I became aware of the smell of the cordite, the vague sound of a child whimpering somewhere, some sort of movement outside beyond Whitaker, and even the dust particles gently floating in the air.

I wanted to kill him.

Whitaker slowly let go of the shotgun with his left hand, spreading his arms wide, holding the shotgun in his right hand. He leaned slowly to his right, and set the shotgun down against the open door. He did it without ever taking his eyes off me. He straightened up.

"Don't look at me," I said. "Put your hands behind your head, lace your fingers together. Now back up slowly toward me. Stop. If you move a finger, I'll kill you. Get on your knees. Cross your feet. Now, face down on the floor."

He started to unlace his fingers.

I kicked him hard in the middle of his back. He smacked the cheap linoleum face down, sprawled out.

"Put your hands behind your head and lace your fingers! Now cross your feet. If you move, at all, I'll send you straight to hell."

I kept the .45 on him as I stepped around him to look out at Tony.

Tony was alive. He was lying on his side out on the ground where he had fallen from the porch. He was squirming and struggling for breath. His shotgun was lying about five feet away.

"Tony, how bad is it."

"Shit!" He swore. "I'm alright. No, I'm not... damn."

I had to keep an eye on Whitaker, so I couldn't do anything to help Tony.

I glanced back outside.

Tony was on his hands and knees now, trying to get to his feet.

I picked up Whitaker's shotgun.

"Tony, I've got Whitaker on the floor." I called out.

Tony was on his feet now, wiping at his eyes.

"Is he still alive? He asked.

"Yes, unarmed and unharmed."

"Well now, isn't that nice?" Tony growled.

CHAPTER 16

The hour after the shooting had flown by. As I secured Whitaker, with Tony's hand cuffs, Tony had read him his rights. Then we cleared the trailer and found the two little girls. They were both alive, but not at all well. They were in an ambulance on the way to the hospital now. Of the two girls, Victoria Winslow was in pretty bad shape. She was conscious, but nearly completely catatonic. It had been the other little girl we had heard scream when Whitaker took the duct tape off her mouth. Tony and I showed up just as he had taken her into a back room in the mobile home

There was no sign of Aaron Horowitz, the little boy who had been with Victoria in the trunk of the Impala.

The whole area was now crawling with emergency vehicles and law enforcement of every conceivable type. There was DPS, sheriff's deputies from two counties, local cops, the Justice of the Peace and constables, even Texas Rangers and game wardens. There was a dispute over jurisdiction.

Tony would be going to the hospital when we were through here. All of the cops were treating him like a hero, with the possible exception of his lieutenant.

Tony looked like hell. I felt that way myself, but Tony was injured. His Kevlar tactical vest had saved his life, stopping all the pellets and debris from the door, but he had taken most of the energy of a twelve-gauge blast full in the chest, from about four feet away. The door had barely slowed the pellets, and he'd been knocked back through the warped, old 2x4 front porch railing, to land on his back in the yard. He'd had splinters and dust from the door in his eyes. His tears had washed away most of it, but splinters and debris had also struck his neck and face.

He had ignored the pain until now, but clearly he was hurt and nearly done in.

"Thanks, J.W. I haven't had a minute to think till now, but I know you saved my life."

"Your vest did that, Tony."

"I'm alive because you kept him from blowing my head off, J.W. If you had stayed on the back porch like I told you to, Whitaker would have killed me."

"Yeah well, the best laid plans don't last past the first contact with the enemy. You wouldn't even have been in harm's way, if I hadn't led you into it. I guess the important point is we got him, and those girls will go home to their families."

"Thanks, J.W., I'm glad to be alive."

Finally! I wished it hadn't taken this to get him there.

We both stared at nothing for a while.

We wanted to forget what we had seen.

Tony had to be driven to the hospital in Tyler. I was taken to the town of Rusk, the County Seat of Cherokee County, for additional questioning. It was routine and according to procedure, but the attitude of the deputies was cordial and as accommodating as they could be.

From a police procedural point of view, this was a disaster. The only saving grace for me was I was a civilian, licensed and legal. I was engaged in investigating the kidnapping of my client's daughter, and I had alerted the authorities. It helped that I had saved Tony's life and secured the suspect. I hadn't even discharged my weapon.

Nothing I had done was worthy of charges, nor would any of my actions interfere with the official investigation. Tony had been in pursuit of a suspect in recent child abductions.

Getting a conviction on Whitaker should be no problem.

My phone was filled with missed calls and recorded messages. I ignored them.

On my way back to Tyler, I called Christine. I told her to call the client in Jacksonville and apologize for my failure to show up for our meeting. I hadn't even thought about it till now.

"The news people have been calling. Somebody must have tipped them off. It's all over the news, John. They're saying an unnamed Tyler police officer located and rescued the two little girls who were abducted from Tyler in the last week. The unnamed officer has been hospitalized with a gunshot injury he sustained while acting on a tip from a citizen. A suspect in the case is in custody. They have a helicopter flying over that mobile home, out there in the woods."

"I think Tony will come out of this in pretty good shape. I don't understand why he was hospitalized. I thought he would just be treated and released"

"What about you, John, are you OK?"

"I'm not hurt, Christine. I'll be fine. Right now I'm pretty shaken up. I think I'll go to the hospital to check on Tony. Tell everybody to leave me alone. I mean, reschedule and take messages. Hell, I don't know what I mean."

"I've got it, John. Don't even think about it."

"Thanks, Christine."

"John, you need to get some rest. You sound terrible, besides they might not let you see Detective Escalante."

Of course, she was right. I was completely wrung out and I wasn't thinking clearly. Every news person in the country would want to interview Tony. The Tyler PD would want to keep him isolated until he was completely debriefed and prepared to meet the press. And since I was involved in the incident, there was no way I could visit him.

"Yeah, OK, I'm going home."

It turned out Tony had been kept for observation to be sure he didn't have a bruised heart. The shotgun blast had fractured his sternum. He had a couple of broken ribs from hitting or landing on the porch railing. His face and neck had small lacerations from the splinters blown out of the door. He was sore, but he would heal.

After what we had seen in that trailer, we both had bruised hearts. You can't live in this world without the occasional bruised or broken heart.

Tony's name and mine eventually got broadcast by the news media as part of the sensational story. I was identified as a private investigator. Tony was always referred to as a hero cop.

The Tyler PD had to go easy on him. He had single-handedly put them in the national spotlight. In fact, because he had already passed his lieutenant's exam, they promoted him to a desk.

Christine and I moved into our fancy new office. I

decided to raise our daily rate to $500.00. We were going to have to generate more income to pay for our new space. Christine was true to her word. She chose the furnishings and appointments with exacting care. Her taste was impeccable.

It was an ideal place to meet with Victoria's parents.

Victoria was... recovering. She was responding well to treatment and was outwardly a typical ten year old girl. She never left her mother's sight these days. Sometimes she woke up at night screaming, but the doctor's felt she would slowly make adjustments and learn to cope. The Winslow family was making plans for home-schooling, starting in the fall.

Children are resilient, thank God.

The door to my corner office was open so Victoria could see her mom, and vice versa. Christine was sitting on the floor with her, playing jacks.

"We can't thank you enough, Mr. Tucker. Lieutenant Escalante said you were responsible for locating Victoria. He said you were the only one who never gave up, and you led him to where that man was keeping the girls."

"Please don't thank me. Thank God. There is another person you can thank as well. His name is Dustin. You may have seen him on the sidewalks at one time or another. He's the tall skinny black man pushing a shopping cart around. He told me everything I needed to know to track down Whitaker."

"Oh, OK, but we hired you. I would like to know what we owe you. Money wise, I mean. We can never repay you what we owe you," Mr. Winslow said.

"You owe me nothing. In fact, here is the check

you first gave me, as a retainer. I'd appreciate it if you would use the money to help Dustin. He's homeless and he has some mental issues. I don't expect miracles, but any help you might give him would go a long way towards doing something good with the money. I would appreciate it, very much."

Eventually we learned the fate of Aaron Horowitz. He was a kid Whitaker had just picked up one day, after visiting his mother in Marshall. The authorities recovered a lot of forensic evidence from both the trailer and the Impala. They found a great deal of further incriminating evidence on Whitaker's computer. He told the police he had sold Aaron Horowitz, to 'some guy from Louisiana' he had connected with over the internet. Whitaker had carried the little boy in the trunk of his Impala, to a truck stop in Shreveport, where he made the sale to a guy he knew only as 'SleeZ362'. It was a Federal offense, transporting a kidnap victim across state lines.

The Feds were able to track down 'SleeZ362' from his internet activities. He was arrested. He led them to the place deep in the Louisiana woods, where he had buried Aaron Horowitz's body. Whitaker was now implicated in the boy's murder.

I took no comfort from the news. It was certainly no comfort to the Horowitz family.

Sometimes, I have to remind myself that this world is not my home.

CHAPTER 17

After our meeting with Victoria and her parents, Christine and I were having pie and coffee in a cafe that had a TV tuned to America's most popular 'talk' show. We found ourselves listening to a conversation on the television, already in progress.

"... It's like the way we all want peace. Everyone everywhere would prefer to live in peace. Peace, at home, at work, in the marketplace, with our neighbors, even inner peace, are all very desirable. But basic human nature is selfish. We are never satisfied. That selfishness guarantees conflict. We want our politicians to agree on a course of action, but they can't compromise because they want to get re-elected. They enjoy the perks and benefits of being career politicians. They put their personal selfish ambition above the good of the country. We can see their selfishness pretty clearly. We're all real quick to point out other people's selfishness, but fail to recognize our own."

"So, you're saying world peace is impossible, because people are selfish?"

"Yes, because we want what we want, and we want it now, on our own terms. Also, we are egotistical. We are convinced our own personal point of view is correct and good, and anyone who disagrees with us is incorrect or 'bad.' We choose up sides, which causes conflict as well. One way or another, it's always 'us versus them'."

"How do we get beyond constantly being in conflict? What will it take, for us to all just get along? If we don't figure it out, then we will simply self-destruct through wars and aggression. The planet can't sustain our rate of population growth, not to mention what we are doing to the environment..."

"Yep, you can always count on "O" asking the hard questions, but never getting to the truth," I said.

"I don't know why you pay any attention, if she irritates you so much," Christine said. "And, you're pretty egotistical yourself. You seem to think you know all the answers," she added.

I smiled. She had a point.

"I guess I just find people fascinating, so intellectually complex and primal, all at the same time. The sheer diversity is astounding. I marvel at the work of God."

"Oh brother," she rolled her eyes. "Here we go again with the God talk. You seem to see your God in everything. I never see God at all. If you can't see it, then it is irrational to believe in it."

"Really, if you can't see it, then it doesn't exist, so it's irrational to believe in it? What if it's invisible to our ocular lenses, or just too small to see, like oxygen or the atom?"

"Don't be ridiculous. You're just being argumentative. Science has proven the existence of oxygen and the atom. You can't prove the existence of God," she said.

"Christine, your test was whether or not a thing could be seen. You said if it couldn't be seen, it must not be real. What if it isn't a question of being invisible or too small to be seen, but rather too complex or too big to be seen?"

"What are you talking about?"

"Some things are too complex or too big to be seen. I'm not talking about the entire cosmos with all of the galaxies and billions of billions of stars, which you haven't seen, though I'll bet you believe it exists. You have seen automobiles built by the Ford Motor Company. Now, those are just creations of Ford. They aren't Ford Motor Company. You could go to a board meeting and see some of the workings of the corporation, but that is only one aspect of the Ford Motor Company. You could be a stockholder, but that is only a small part of Ford. The FMC is just too big and complex for you to see it all, at any one time, or in any one place. So is the Federal Government," I continued. "We see what it does, but we don't see the government itself. These things are just man made constructs. How much more diverse and complex are the works of God? Just His works, mind you. God himself is far bigger and more complex than our eyes are able to see, or our minds are able to grasp. Science hasn't proven His existence in the whole. However, science is constantly discovering more and more, about the complexity of His creation. Humans are only able to speculate about how big the cosmos is, and that's only a tiny part of His creation." I was just starting to warm up. "To look around us at the things we see on the earth and in the heavens and say we can't see God, is like a single bacterium on the back of an elephant, saying the elephant doesn't exist, because it can't see the elephant. It's not really a seeing problem, it's a believing problem. No matter how smart the bacterium is, I'll bet it's not as smart as the elephant, and God created both of them."

Christine blinked at me.

"Honestly John, do you sit up at night thinking about this stuff?"

I grinned at her.

When we got back to the office, my part-time operative, Gary, came in with his report on an insurance fraud case.

"It's all there in the log book, John. I think this guy is legitimately injured. I watched him for days. He hasn't left the house much. He can't play with his kids. I saw him try to lift a bag of groceries out of the back of his wife's car. He couldn't do it. I could see he was frustrated and embarrassed. I have video of it. If you combine what I've seen with the medical reports and the anecdotal information from people who know him, it all adds up."

I nodded.

"Good work. I'll wrap it up with the client. I have something else for you."

"Yeah, goody, goody, what is it?"

"This one is a domestic issue. Christine took the particulars. We need to gather some information on one Timothy Leroy Shaw, 29 years old."

"Not another divorce case! I thought we were pretty much through with those."

"No, this is more of a character assessment. Apparently Mr. Shaw has made some threats against the brother of his girlfriend. The brother is hiring us. He's concerned for his safety and the safety of his sister. Christine gathered some basic background on Mr. Shaw, but I need you to follow him around for a while and see what he's into."

"I can't start on it until Wednesday."

"Not a problem, I'll handle it till then. I'll pass it off to you on Wednesday, if it isn't already concluded."

Tim Shaw's history showed he had no felony convictions, DWI's, or any arrest record. He had no restraining orders against him and he wasn't a registered sex offender.

His credit report was pretty typical for a 29 year old. He had served as a corporal in the Marine Corps. He had never been married. He worked as an electrician for a company that did mostly commercial jobs. On paper, he looked pretty harmless.

I decided to check out the girlfriend, Diane Montgomery, and her brother, Tom Montgomery, as well. When they came up clean I was back to square one.

"Christine, tell me again about the Tim Shaw case. What's the issue exactly?"

"A guy by the name of Tom Montgomery called in and requested our services. Tom Montgomery is about 30 years old, and his sister, Diane Montgomery, is 22. He said his sister is dating this guy, Tim Shaw, and his sister, Diane, thinks they are in love and will get married." She began. "Mr. Montgomery claims he heard from a friend that Tim Shaw is a well-known player, and is only interested in putting notches on his bed post. He decided to confront Tim Shaw about these allegations. When he did, Mr. Shaw told him to mind his own business and keep his mouth shut. Mr. Montgomery claims Shaw threatened to kill him if he said anything to his sister about the matter." She concluded.

"It's a crime to threaten violence against someone, but since there were no witnesses..." Gary trailed off.

"... Exactly. That's why he decided to hire us to check out Mr. Shaw. He hopes to get something conclusive against him that he can take to his sister. He doesn't want to risk doing anything which might put him crossways with Mr. Shaw. He believes Shaw was serious about killing him," Christine said.

"Yeah, but if we do find anything Mr. Montgomery can use against him, Shaw is going to know

Montgomery was involved. Then what happens?"

"I guess he's hoping we find something criminal, so he can get Shaw put away."

"Sounds like a good way to get into trouble with his sister. The heart wants what the heart wants. Diane might hate her brother for interfering." I pointed out.

"Not if she doesn't know about it." Christine answered.

"Oh. Did you agree to keep the investigation a secret from the sister?"

"Uh, look, this is all new to me, John. Did I make a mistake? Mr. Montgomery added that last part, when he brought me the check for the retainer."

Since my name had been all over the news, we had been swamped with calls. Christine had handled it all with her usual grace and style. The guidelines I had given her about what kind of case we would or would not take, or what considerations were important, hadn't covered anything like this.

"No, Christine, you didn't make a mistake. I just needed to know I shouldn't talk openly to Diane Montgomery about the investigation. I didn't understand that, when you first told me the story. Is there anything else I should know?"

"Diane Montgomery is pregnant," she said.

Since I had decided to re-connect cameras to the brackets in the hallways, it made sense to call an electrician. It was a simple, four camera CCTV system that would be easy for me to install all by myself, but I would arrange to have Tim Shaw be the electrician sent to us to do the job. It would be more convenient for us to observe him up close in the workplace.

"... Yes sir, I'm ready to install the three dome cameras in the hallway. One camera will be directly above the office entrance, facing down the hall toward the elevators and the stairwell, the other two at each end of the short hallway, facing toward the one above the door. You'll be able to see anyone or anything approaching this office from any direction. Where do you want the fourth camera?" Tim Shaw asked.

"I want it directly behind and above Christine's desk in the reception area. I want to be able to see anyone who comes in the front door," I replied.

"John! That's creepy. I'll feel like you are constantly looking over my shoulder," Christine said.

"It might be annoying at first, but once you get used to it, you won't even think about it. With the system set up this way, we can monitor the pictures from our computers or our smart phones, and we'll have a digital record of everything."

"Mr. Tucker, do you want separate monitors so you can have a constant picture of the hallways?"

"No, Tim, we don't need to constantly watch the hallways. The cameras are mostly to record the traffic in and out of the office, and keep the honest people honest. No one will be able to break into the office without being recorded. They can't steal the recordings, because they are being digitally recorded directly to a separate data processor they won't be able to find."

"OK, I'll get started. I'll need to get up into the ceiling behind your desk Ms. Valakova. I'd like to start there and get that camera set up, so I'm out of your way as quickly as possible."

"OK, how much time do you need? And please call me Christine."

"Yes, ma'am, I mean Christine. I'll need at least thirty minutes, to mount the camera and run the cables."

"Wow, you're fast. You must really know what you're doing."

Christine was playing her part well.

"It's really pretty simple to do, ma'am. The most time-consuming part will be mounting the camera," Tim said.

"Will I be in your way if I hang out in here with you? I'll use my laptop, so I don't really need to be at my desk," she asked, demurely.

I was impressed and surprised. For a woman who didn't like to be touched or flirted with, she was pretty good at turning on the charm.

"No ma'am. I'll try not to get a lot of dust and debris on your desk top."

I caught Christine's eye. She nodded.

"I've got to go out for a little while, I'll be back in about an hour," I said.

"OK, see you later," Christine said, smiling a big, million candle watt smile.

I was on my way to interview Tim Shaw's landlady. I had only driven a few blocks, when I got that old familiar feeling. Something was wrong.

Christine answered her cell phone on the second ring. She was fine, no problems there. What I had seen or heard, now alerting me to danger?

It was my rear-view mirror.

Behind me, was a big black SUV which had followed me out of the parking lot from my office building. There was nothing odd about that. My office was in one of a pair of high rise buildings. The parking lot was a busy place, with lots of traffic coming and going. In Texas, big SUVs are as ubiquitous as ball caps or cowboy boots. The SUV could have been going in the same direction as I was. I had only made one turn.

It was time for another turn.

Without signaling, I took the next available right turn. I immediately found myself in a residential neighborhood. Watching my mirror, I saw the black SUV come around the corner behind me. Now it was getting more interesting. I decided to play follow the leader for a while.

CHAPTER 18

Big, black SUVs are pretty much the first choice of government agencies. I was the new tenant in a space previously occupied by a government agency. Maybe that was the connection to the vehicle following me. Then again, anybody could buy a black SUV.

Who were these guys?

After a half mile or so, I made another right turn. The SUV didn't follow me.

Was I just paranoid? Sometimes I wondered.

Then again, "just because you're paranoid, it doesn't mean people aren't out to get you".

I drove on to the apartments where Tim Shaw lived. The SUV didn't follow me.

His landlady was a wealth of information. She clearly had her nose in everybody's business. She told me his habits, complained about the way he bagged his trash, even suggested Mr. Shaw needed a new set of tires on his car. She talked about his girlfriend Diane Montgomery. In all of my lengthy listening, she never indicated there was anything remotely sinister about Tim Shaw, or his friends.

As I was leaving her apartment, I spotted another big black SUV, parked up the street. It could be just another example of my paranoid leanings, because as I say, SUVs of every kind are as common as birds, in this town. Still, I decided to drive by it.

It was the same one. I recognized the license number.

Now, what are the odds…?

When I got back to the office, Tim Shaw was out in the hall, up on a ladder, installing the second camera.

"Hey Tim, how's it coming along?"

"No problems, Mr. Tucker. This is really pretty much routine. We should be able to test the system in another hour or so."

I nodded and went inside.

"Well, did you learn anything? I've got nothing. He seems like a pretty decent guy," I said.

"… Same here. When he finally became aware I was flirting with him, he started talking about his girlfriend. He was always polite, never forward or sexually aggressive. I think he really is in love with his girlfriend. He enjoyed talking about her. He doesn't seem like the same guy Tom Montgomery told me about. I didn't see anything that would cause me any concern whatsoever."

I thought about what this might mean.

I also thought about the SUV.

I borrowed Christine's car and went for a spin. No one followed me. After explaining the situation, I sent Christine out in my truck to go to Starbuck's and bring back some coffee for the three of us.

When she got back, she was pale. After Tim took his coffee back out into the hallway, Christine told me the story.

"It was just like you described it. I didn't see them follow me from here, but when I came out of the Starbuck's, they were parked a couple of rows away. They followed me back here."

"Did you get a good look at the driver?"

"No, there were always a couple of cars between us."

"Did they get a good look at you?"

She nodded.

I could see she was concerned.

"This isn't about you. They were following my truck. They either have a tracking device on it, or they're accessing the GPS system in the truck. That way they don't need to sit here and watch for me. If the truck starts moving, they can go right to wherever it is, or drive along on another road running parallel to it, and follow without being seen at all."

"These days, everything from our cell phones to our cars is connected to GPS and emergency services, which can be used as locaters, who would bother to install a transponder on your truck? Do you think it could be the police or FBI? I know the NSA and FBI do that to persons of interest. I saw on TV, where some Muslim guy was trying to sue the Feds for breach of privacy, after they put a tracking device on his car."

"No, I don't think it's the Feds or the police, they could legally use the GPS in my truck. Private persons wouldn't be able to access it, so they would have to install their own."

"Who are they, and why are they following you?" she asked.

Good question.

"I don't know, but I intend to find out."

Later, as I was sitting at my desk, I tried to puzzle it out. I was pretty sure they weren't Feds. There was no reason for Feds to be following me. Actually, there was no reason for anyone to be following me. If they weren't Feds, then who were they?

Christine buzzed me in my office. The security cameras were all hooked up, and ready for testing.

Tim showed us how, using our computers, we could see the pictures from all four cameras on one screen, or we could select which camera angle we preferred. We could even zoom in on an image, without much distortion.

"Y'all can access the feed on your smartphones or your home computer. So, if you want to watch absolutely nothing happening at three in the morning, you can." He chuckled.

When he was gone, Christine and I agreed there was something strange about this case.

There are a number of ways to deal with having a tracking device on your vehicle. You have to determine your goals. Do you want to avoid being tracked? You could abandon the car with the tracking device in favor of another. That will work well for brief outings. Eventually they'll track the new vehicle. You could remove the device and either destroy it or throw it into a dumpster. I like the latter for setting them up to track the trash truck.

If your goal is to find out who is tracking you, you can lead them into a trap and confront them head on.

I like to track the trackers. They seldom consider that while they are following someone, someone may be following them.

The quickest and easiest way is to follow them as they follow your vehicle, with someone else driving it. Or, you remove the device and put it on a different vehicle and follow them as they follow the decoy. Pizza delivery vehicles, taxi cabs, and rental vehicles are good for that. I might even go with a parcel delivery truck.

I got a call from Tom Montgomery, asking if I had found any leads yet, into the nefarious character of Timothy Leroy Shaw.

"No Mr. Montgomery. I've run a background check on him, and I've interviewed people who know him. I'm arranging to have surveillance put on him, but we have nothing at this time. I would have to say the investigation is 'ongoing.' I should remind you our fee is $500.00 per day. You have paid us a retainer of one thousand dollars. We've pretty much used that up, and we have nothing, so far. I can't guarantee we will find anything suspect on the subject. I will be happy to submit a written report on the findings of our investigation to this point. I'll understand if you don't want to commit to additional expense. Full time surveillance is one of the most time consuming and therefor expensive services we offer."

He was thinking about what I'd said. I could tell he hadn't expected my answer.

"No, no, the expense is not a problem. I need you to find anything, anything at all, that will show my sister how nasty he really is. You said you were going to follow him around, right?"

"Sometimes, surveillance will lead to interesting contacts and activities."

"Yeah, yeah, do it, and send me a bill! Thanks."

He hung up.

Now I had some answers.

CHAPTER 19

Tony and I were too busy to practice our shooting for more than a month. We'd both been swamped with work in the aftermath of the Winslow/Whitaker case. Tony also needed time to heal. We figured out a good time for both of us and met at the indoor range on the SW Loop, where we were both members.

"So, Tony, now that you're a lieutenant, have they figured out what division to assign you to?"

"Robbery/homicide for now, but we all float wherever we're most needed depending on our case load, same as always."

I whistled.

"I always knew you were the best detective in that division. Congratulations."

"Yeah well, we'll see."

"What's the problem?"

He was silent for a moment, as he pushed .40 caliber rounds into a clip.

"I never wanted to be a paper pusher. I don't think I'm very good at conducting meetings. I don't like having to try to figure out the politics of the job. I know I'm going to have to face some TV cameras again. There's just a lot more busy-work than I'm used to, and I don't like being 'the Boss.'"

"Heavy is the head that wears the crown." I suggested.

He smiled.

"On the other hand, I like the pay grade, and because I'm always on call, I get more flexibility with my schedule."

"It's good to be the king." I agreed.

We both grinned

"How do y'all like your new office?"

"You should come by and see it. Our door is always open to those who protect and serve."

"... Donuts, do you have any donuts? I like donuts." Tony said, wringing his hands.

We both shot better than we expected to. I was concerned about the occasional 'flyer.' Out of fifty shots, I had six rounds hit the target outside the ten ring. They were kind of random in their placement. I couldn't be sure if it was caused by my ammunition or my shooting.

"It's a poor workman who blames his tools," Tony observed.

When we got outside, I saw the SUV parked a few rows away from where I had parked.

Tony and I are both in the habit of scanning everything around us, wherever we are. We're not really looking for anything; we're just staying aware of everything. The process is sometimes referred to as "soft or hard eyes". "Soft" eyes look at the big picture, while "hard" eyes focus on specific subjects, movement, or details.

Tony noticed when I focused on the SUV for a second. He saw me frown.

"Is there a problem, J.W.?"

"I don't know Tony, probably not, but that SUV has been following me, for days."

"You want me to run the plate?"

I looked at him, and chuckled.

"I thought you made it pretty clear, you're not my conduit of data from the DMV."

He nodded.

"I'm sorry I snapped at you. I know you won't abuse my trust, or my position. If I can help you, I will, J.W."

I thought about it for a moment.

"I appreciate your faith in me. How's your faith in God?"

He grinned.

"It's growing. Do you want my help or not?"

"Naw, I think I'll get this figured out on my own. Thanks, though, Tony."

Tom Montgomery had asked us to do some surveillance, so we were doing as he asked. I had assigned Gary to do the surveillance. He had been watching the subject since Wednesday. Using a directional boom mike, mounted on a video camera, Gary recorded and filmed a meeting with a man in a suit and tie. I was watching the video of the two men walking down the street.

Man in suit: "How's it going?"

Subject: "He's still working it. I just got him started watching him."

Man in suit: "How long will that continue?"

Subject: "I don't know, but not long. There's probably nothing to see."

Man in suit: "Can you get him to go to a particular place, at a particular time?"

Subject: "Probably, it might depend on where and why."

A car went by in front of the camera, and the microphone recorded the sound of the car.

Man in suit: "… him that… will be…"

Another car went by in front of the camera, and

the microphone only picked up the sound of that car.

Man in suit: "I'll call you with the details. Just get him there."

They walked a few more feet to the corner, where they parted company. Gary continued to watch the subject until he returned to his parked car.

I considered what I had just watched.

The meeting had been strictly business. It had been held outdoors in a public setting. The two men barely looked at each other, and could have been just a couple of businessmen, casually meeting as they walked down the street. The whole segment of video lasted less than five minutes. The conversation only lasted fifty two seconds.

It told me everything I needed to know.

The subject was Tom Montgomery. He was working for the man in the suit.

I knew the man in the suit.

I would have to revisit a previous case.

As it turned out, I had to postpone the visit because of my next appointment.

Mr. and Mrs. Drew Murphy were good people who tried to be good parents, but their daughter was not the sharpest tool in the shed. Like many girls her age, she thought she was all grown up.

She thought wrong.

It can take a lifetime to grow up. Sometimes people grow old along the way. Sometimes they don't get the chance to grow up, or grow old. Some mistakes are fatal. Lori Murphy made a mistake, she fell in love.

Her 20 year old "boyfriend" turned out to be a loser and abuser. At sixteen years old, Lori woke up in Dallas, wondering how she had let him pimp her out. She had called home only once. She was in dire straits.

"We just want her to come home."

"Yes ma'am, I understand. Does she want to come home? How do y'all imagine this will turn out?"

Mrs. Murphy was quiet for a moment.

It's hard for a parent to clearly see. Parents love. Parents sacrifice. Parents provide, but it can be hard for a parent to see. A parent's vision can be clouded by their dreams for the future and their memories of the past.

"We understand what you're saying. We're hoping she's realized her mistake, and really does want to come home," her dad said.

Parents also hope.

Love hopes.

"OK. Here's the thing. I can find your daughter. I can bring her home to you, but I can't promise she'll stay. I can't promise she'll be the same girl y'all remember. She may be damaged in ways we can't predict. She may need professional medical, spiritual and/or psychiatric help. If you understand what I've told you, and you're willing to take the chance, I'll take the case. But, I repeat, I can't make any promises about who the girl will be, when I bring her back to Tyler."

"She's our baby girl. What would you do?"

My mission on earth had prevented me from experiencing the joys and sorrows of being a parent. My time on earth had exposed me to generations of parents.

"OK, I just wanted to make sure you both understand the implications and complications of this course of action."

"What else can we do?"

"You could just wait. Maybe she will come home on her own."

They looked at each other and then down at the floor.

"She can't. She told us she wants to come home,

but that man won't let her. He watches her constantly. She's afraid, I mean really terrified. She sounds awful. She sounds like she's given up," her mom said.

"Have you contacted the Dallas police?"

"We did. They were very understanding. They said they saw this kind of thing far too often. They promised to look for her, and said they would call us when they found her. That was ten days ago."

I nodded, and said, "They have officers who are familiar with the streets and the girls working them. They'll do what they can. It could take some time. If she's not still in Dallas, if she's in Ft. Worth, Arlington, or some other part of the Metroplex, the word may not get out."

My first step was to call the Dallas P.D.

CHAPTER 20

"Sergeant Jacobs here, what can I do for you?"

"Sergeant, my name is John Wesley Tucker. I'm a Private Investigator here in Tyler. Your name was given to me by your LT. He suggested you might be able to bring me up to speed on a runaway I'm looking for."

"OK. What is the subject's name, sex and age?"

"Her name is Lori Murphy, she's just turned sixteen. About three months ago she ran away with her boyfriend. His name is Orlando Cruz. Her parents contacted your department about ten days ago, as soon as they learned of her whereabouts."

I could hear fingers flying over computer keys.

"Yeah, OK, here it is. We have a BOLO on her. Nothing reported so far. What can I do for you?"

"Have you, or can you crosscheck for 'Jane Does' at the morgue."

I could hear her fingers flying again, behind her voice.

"I can tell you... there is no Jane Doe matching her description, in either the Dallas County or the Tarrant County morgues."

That was a relief.

"Do you have any other information I might find useful?"

"Not really, Mr. Tucker. These girls drift from one area to another. They change their appearance. They get hooked on drugs. Unless we pick her up on drug charges or a soliciting for prostitution charge, we probably won't find her."

"I'll be coming to Dallas to find her, and return her to her parents. I'm just giving y'all a 'heads up' notice."

It took me several hours of research, but I found an address for Orlando Cruz. Apparently he didn't feel any need to hide his identity or his whereabouts.

Because I didn't want to be tailed to and from Dallas by a big black SUV, I rented a car for the trip. It was an ugly, little, economy car, with New York license plates. I got the extra insurance.

Orlando and Lori 'lived' in a ratty, little apartment complex in south Oak Cliff, a Dallas suburb.

At about 2:30 the next morning, I was waiting for them when they got in.

I had already had a little run-in with the local thugs. After knocking on the door of apartment 221, at about midnight, I was sitting at the top of the stairs on the second floor of the apartment building. Some young guys, who were built like football linemen, but dressed like hip hop artists, took exception to my presence. They indicated they intended to cause me some level of personal discomfort. It was prevented from escalating into a big scene, by me showing them my old DHS credentials and my .45. The credentials were outdated, the .45 wasn't. I held the high ground, so although there were a lot of harsh words and hand signals, and one of them showed me his gun, they shuffled away acting tough, a couple of them holding their pants up by the crotch, with one hand.

I continued waiting on the grungy second floor. Most of the families in the building had gone to bed. I knew the thugs were around and probably watching me, but they didn't feel lucky enough to push the point.

I had just decided to come back in daylight, when an old beaten up, green, two door sedan drove into the parking lot. I eased back into the deep shadows at the end of the building. Someone had broken out the security light.

Shortly, Orlando and Lori came staggering up the stairs. It took Orlando a full minute to get the key into the lock and the door open. Apparently the lock kept swimming out of his reach. He and Lori managed to get through the door opening without falling. They didn't see me coming. I walked in right behind Lori. The stink in there was nearly overpowering.

I didn't wait. I hit Orlando with a flat leather sap I was carrying in my pocket. He went down and out, as if someone had let all the air out of him. Lori just stood there staring. She had a kind of vacant look.

Frisking Orlando, in a pocket I found three hundred dollars, all in tens and twenties. He also had a cheap switchblade and a J-frame, .38 revolver. I stuck the gun behind my waistband and put the knife and cash in my pocket. I grabbed Lori by the arm and directed her out the door and down the stairs. She didn't resist. It was as if she was used to being pushed and pulled around. We went to the car and I got her buckled into the passenger seat. I had almost made it around to the driver's side, when the band of hip hop linemen showed up again.

There were five of them. One had a baseball bat and another was swinging a golf club, so maybe they really were athletes.

"Where you takin' da bitch? The spokesman asked. He had a grill of gold over his front teeth. I think one of those teeth had a diamond in it.

I had seen them coming, so I had the roll of money in my hand.

"We're going for a drive if that's cool with you."

"Hell man, you ain't no kinda fed, that ain't no police car, and you ain't goin' nowhere," another one said.

I held up the roll of money.

"There's three hundred dollars here, I expect it'll pay the toll."

I handed the first speaker the roll of money. The attention of the others was drawn to the bills as he started counting it. I took the opportunity to duck into the driver's seat, real quick like. As I started the car, one of them jerked my door open.

"You ain't goin' nowhere mo..." he stopped speaking, because he was looking into the muzzle of my .45.

"Step off, or the last thing you ever hear will be a real loud noise, and then the rest of us will all start shooting each other."

He took a step back. They were all poised to attack.

I managed to shift the car into reverse without letting go of my gun, but I had to look away from them for a second to do it. 'Grill boy' pulled a gun out of his pants, as the two 'sportsmen' started pounding on the car with the bat and the golf club. The windshield on Lori's side was smashed and crazed, as I stepped on the gas and shot backwards out from between them, managing to turn the car and accelerate backwards toward the street. Gun fire erupted as two or three of them fired rapid shots at us. In the middle of the street now, I turned and continued accelerating backward away from the apartment building. They came running out into the street, and poured gunfire at us. I heard the occasional bullet hit the car. Within seconds, we were three blocks away. I whipped the car around and took off fast, grateful they had not managed to shoot out the tires.

I looked over at Lori, concerned she might have been shot. She looked terribly frightened now, but did not appear to be bleeding. A couple of blocks later, I came to a well-lit gas station and pulled in. I jumped out and ran around to the passenger side, pulled open the door and confirmed that Lori had not been hit. Neither had I.

The car was another story. I could see around and between the cracks in the windshield, but only on my side. The passenger side of the windshield was nearly bashed in and was completely shattered. There was a single bullet hole in it, up high. The driver side headlight was shot out. The side windows were crazed and shattered and there was glass all over the back seat. There were bullet holes high in the driver's side quarter panels and there were bashes and dents from the bat and the golf club.

I was as amazed the car was still running, as I was that we were alive. It was grace and mercy for us; those guys were just firing wildly and not aiming. Otherwise, I would surely be dead and Lori might be as well. As I walked around the car, only nine bullet holes could be counted. Some bullets had passed right through the car, doing a lot of body damage. A couple had ricocheted through the roof and the back seat. Other than the one headlight, they had failed to hit the radiator or anything else vital, not even a tire. They must have fired at least twenty five rounds between them.

I jumped back in the car and took off. I knew there was a pretty good chance they would pursue me in their own vehicle. I was surprised I could hear no sirens or see any cops yet.

A couple of minutes later, we drove onto I-20 and headed east. As I went under an overpass, I saw the flashing blue and red lights of police cars, flying by overhead. I kept going. Looking at my watch, I was astonished to see less than four minutes had passed since I had put Lori in the passenger seat. Adrenaline had slowed the rest of the world down.

I cursed myself for a fool. I had nearly gotten myself and Lori killed. What was I thinking? This could have been handled differently.

It would be a long drive to Tyler, and I was experiencing the let-down of the adrenaline wearing off. I was getting dangerously sleepy, having to force myself to remain alert.

I couldn't stop checking the rear-view mirror.

CHAPTER 21

"Where are you taking me?" Lori asked, thickly.

I looked at her. She was still high or drunk or both, but she was alert enough to be afraid.

"Home, Lori, I'm taking you back to your family."

She considered that for a moment, and then her countenance crumbled. She shook her head.

"I can never go home again," she sobbed. "Please turn around."

Tears were streaming down her face. She buried her face in her hands.

"No, Lori, it'll be OK. Don't worry. We'll be in Tyler in a couple of hours."

When she looked up again her expression was calculated.

"Come on baby, if you turn around, I'll make it worth your while. Whatever you want, just turn around and I'll do you right here." She put her hand on my thigh.

She was trying to look seductive, but her face was somewhat slackened by whatever chemicals she had ingested and her cheap, pink wig was crooked and messed up. Her face was streaked with make-up and tears. Under all of that were the frightened eyes of a barely sixteen year old girl, now hardened and desperate.

"Stop it," I snapped.

She pulled back away from me and sneered.

"What, you're gay? You like boys? I can hook you up."

"Lori, do you have any idea how much you are loved?"

She laughed. "Oh, mister, you have no idea how much I've been 'loved'."

I gritted my teeth.

After a few minutes she tried another tactic.

"If you don't pull over and let me out, right now, I'll tell people you raped me."

I ignored her.

"Please mister. Just stop the car and let me out. I'll be fine."

"Why don't you want to go home, Lori?"

She looked out the window on her side for a little while. "Look at me. Don't you get it?" she pleaded.

I nodded.

"Doesn't matter,"

"You don't get it. You don't know what I am, what I've done. How can I ever go back to my family or my friends?"

"You are God's child, and He loves you."

"Oh, you're a preacher. Hallelujah! Praise the Lord, and pass the offering plate."

"Do I look like a preacher?"

She stared at me for a moment.

"Are you a cop?"

"No ma'am."

"Who are you?"

"My name is John Wesley Tucker. Your parents hired me to find you and bring you home. They love you very much. They know what you've been through, at least some of it, and they want you home and safe."

Her lip quivered and she looked at me intently. "How can I ever be safe? Orlando will come after me. Now my family will be in danger! I don't know what he'll do to me!" She wailed.

"Orlando has no idea where you are. He was asleep on the floor when we left. If his friends describe this car, it has New York license plates. If he does come to Tyler, looking for you, he'll find me. He won't like that."

"What am I supposed to do?"

I looked at her and smiled.

"Live, Lori. Finish growing up, finish school, have a healthy, normal life."

She was quiet for a time.

"Do you really think I can, mister?"

I smiled again.

"I know you can. Your parents will do whatever it takes to help you get it sorted out. So will I."

"I just don't think I can."

I nodded. "It's nearly 3:30 in the morning, you've been through hell. You're beaten down and wiped out. No wonder you don't think you can. Have a little faith, Lori. If not in yourself, then have faith in God. You're right, you know, you probably can't do it by yourself, but you don't have to. You'll see. Just relax and watch for the miracle."

She shook her head. "That's easy for you to say."

We drove on in silence for a while.

We got back to Tyler just before 5:00 AM.

I took Lori directly to her parents. After the initial wake up and shock of having her home, after all the coffee, tears and prayers, I left them with instructions to call me if there was a complication. By "complication" I meant Orlando Cruz.

It was 6:15 when I got back to my apartment.

I would have to charge Lori's parents for two days work.

When I got to the office, I told Christine about Lori.

"The poor girl, how will she ever get over something like that?"

"Earlier this morning, she became a Christian. She's born again. God will heal her and direct her paths."

Christine rolled her eyes.

"There you go again. 'God loves you and has a wonderful plan for your life'," She mocked. "Would it be the same loving God who let that jackass take her away from her family and pimp her out? Was that his wonderful plan for her life? Is it the same loving God who causes horrific storms, and earthquakes, destroying thousands of people's lives? Is it the loving God who unleashes pestilence and disease on his children, or sits by idly watching babies starve to death?"

"Christine, God doesn't cause those things. We all live on the same violent planet. This is a fallen and dangerous world. The things you mention are all caused by our separation from God. The sin of man has led to the sickness of the whole creation. In this case, Lori put herself in a bad situation. Yes, God let her do it. He lets us all make our own choices, and we get to live with the consequences of our choices. He also forgives His children when we sin. He sent a Redeemer to pay the ultimate and final penalty, His only son. How much more loving can He be?"

She shook her head.

"You Christians believe you are the only ones this 'loving God' of yours will let into heaven. Everyone else gets sent to hell."

"Not exactly, Christine, God doesn't desire that anyone should go to hell. Hell is meant for the enemies of God, those who oppose Him. Some people think all people are God's children. That is simply not the case. God's children are those who acknowledge Him as their father in heaven. He simply offers the gift of salvation through Jesus to anyone and everyone who will receive it. People get to choose, to accept the gift or to reject it. Anyone may come to Him and be adopted as His child. Anyone may choose not to come to Him. Heaven or hell, they get to choose the destination for themselves."

"It isn't fair John. Why do the innocent suffer? Why do the wicked prosper? If your God is such a good guy, why does he sit around and do nothing, as decent people waste away to cancer, and let us kill each other, while we poison the planet?"

I nodded. I felt the same pain. There is horror all around us.

"If there is no God, as you seem to presume, then everything in life is random. If there is a God, by definition, He is different from us. He is more than we are capable of understanding, well beyond our judgment, or our limitations. You expect fairness, according to your definition. He won't fit into any box made by any ordinary human being. Why do you think you have a right to be the one to judge a holy God?"

"Well, you seem to think you have God all figured out. You are the only one who 'gets him'."

"No, that's not it at all. I've known Him a long time. The only thing I'm sure of is I don't 'get' Him. I'm not capable of it. He constantly surprises me. He does things in ways that are hard for me to understand. That's my limitation, not His error. I fail to hear His voice sometimes. Should He yell louder, so I can hear Him?"

She stared at me for a moment.

"No, John, He just needs to speak loud enough for me to hear Him."

I smiled.

"He is speaking to you. You'll hear Him soon enough."

Later that morning, I was sitting in my office

working on a fourth cup of coffee, when Christine buzzed me.

"You have a visitor. Lieutenant Escalante, of the Tyler Police Department is here to see you."

I checked the monitor. Sure enough, there was a clear picture of Tony, smiling at Christine.

"Well, send him on in," I drawled.

"Nice digs, J.W.," Tony said, by way of greeting. "That redhead is stunning."

He sat down in one of the chairs upholstered in green fabric with hunt scenes that now sat in front of my shiny new carved oak desk.

I grinned.

"That's Christine, and she did it all, Tony. She found this office, negotiated the deal, and decorated it herself. All I do around here is work to earn the money. She even opens the mail and pays the bills."

"How can you possibly deserve all this?"

I shrugged.

"What brings you by, LT?"

"It's business, actually. It seems we got a call from a local car rental agency this morning. They wanted to report their suspicion one of their cars might have been used in connection with a crime."

I groaned.

"When our officer arrived to look at the vehicle, he found it shot to pieces. Further investigation revealed you were the man who rented the car. Is this correct?"

"Good thing I got the extra insurance," I offered.

He scowled.

I shrugged.

"Well, I did get surprisingly good gas mileage."

"J.W., tell me you didn't use the car in connection with a crime."

I told him the whole story.

"I can't believe you were able to drive that wreck

all the way back to Tyler. You only had one head-light, and part of the windshield was shattered. You could have hit a deer or gotten a ticket."

"Here's the thing, Tony. That guy, Orlando, may show up here in Tyler. If he does, he'll try to take her back."

"It's a little late for you to be thinking about what he might do. I looked at the rental car. There were nine bullet entrance holes in it and six exit holes. The car is smashed and battered. It's a miracle you survived. Why didn't you just have the Dallas PD arrest him?"

"Arrest him for what, Tony, statutory rape? She wouldn't have cooperated with the police. She's terrified of him."

He considered my perspective for a moment.

"It sounds like he probably has a record. I'll look into it. His friends are probably gangstas; I'll look into that as well. This is the second time you've been shot at, in what, two months? Did you shoot anybody?"

I shook my head.

"Good, I suspect you're probably guilty of dis-turbing the peace, up there in Oak Cliff, but that's their problem."

He reached behind his back and drew my Browning Hi Power from his waistband, and hand-ed it to me.

"I know you've been missing this. We don't need it anymore, so there you go. Use it in good health," he smirked.

I grinned.

"There's something else. I looked up the license number on the black SUV, which you said has been following you. Would you like to know who it's registered to?"

I was shocked!

"Tony, I didn't ask you to…"

He held up a hand.

"Forget it, J.W. Do you want to know, or not?"

"I think I already know."

"Yeah, who do you think it is?"

I put my finger tips together and considered what I had seen on the video footage.

"Is it a guy by the name of Walter Farley?"

Tony shook his head. "Nope, I've never heard of him."

"You're kidding. I could have sworn it would be him."

Tony shook his head again.

"Sorry, Sherlock, the car is registered to the World Wide Security Agency."

CHAPTER 22

I hate summer in East Texas. The heat is often oppressive. It's common for it to be at least one hundred degrees Fahrenheit, and about 90% humidity. Fortunately, summer only lasts from about May through September, five months, more or less.

It was now full on summer in Tyler, Texas. The temp was 103°. The Crepe Myrtles were fading, and the sound of the air conditioners could be heard in the land.

I learned a good deal more about Walter Farley. I had all of his records, including his service record. Before he started working for Simpson Oil and Gas Company, he had worked for a competing oil and gas company in Oklahoma. Before that, he had been in the Army. He had done a tour in Afghanistan. He had been an intelligence specialist.

He was probably also a sociopath.

It's hard to identify a true sociopath. They become experts at deceiving others.

Sociopaths have no sense of guilt. They don't conform to the rules of society out of any sense of moral duty. They only pretend to conform, to avoid getting caught. They are incapable of understanding moral behavior. They are focused on themselves, and getting what they want. There are no limits to what they will do to satisfy themselves. From the time they are children they begin learning to cover their tracks and throw suspicion on someone else. They are masterful deceivers and manipulators.

Deception and lies had been Walter's problem in the Army. He had an honorable discharge, but his service record indicated he had tried to manipulate the system and was repeatedly caught in lies.

In some ways lies and deception might seem like a good thing for an intelligence specialist, but in combat the facts are essential. Military intelligence is all about gathering data, analyzing the data and making decisions based on the analysis.

If the data is unreliable, if the facts cannot be confirmed, lives may be lost. I had been in combat situations where unreliable intelligence got people killed.

Walter was unreliable. He had been caught fabricating intelligence to make himself look good.

I had more digging to do.

I was thinking about the implications of what I had learned, when Christine buzzed me.

"John, I think you'll want to take this call. It's Lori Murphy. She's frantic."

I punched the button on my phone.

"Hey, Lori, what's up?"

"Mr. Tucker, h he f f found me!" she cried.

"Easy now, who found you, Orlando?"

"Yes," she sobbed. "I answered the ph ph phone and it was him. He, he knows I'm heeeeeere."

I knew it wouldn't do any good for me to remind her I had specifically instructed her not to answer the phone, for this very reason.

"OK, calm down. Do you know where he is?"

"N n no, but he knows where I am. He'll come here and g get me."

"No, he won't. We won't let that happen. I'm on my way over there, right now, and I'll have the police watch your house. Make sure all the doors and windows are locked. Where are your parents?"

"They, they're at work. I c called my dad. He t t told me to c call you. He's c coming h home t too."

"Lori, listen to me! Calm down. I need you to hang up the phone, and make sure the house is locked up and secure. Do you understand?"

"Yes sir."

"OK. I'll be there in fifteen minutes."

I hung up the phone, grabbed my Jacket and headed out through the front office. Christine had grabbed her purse.

"I'm coming with you," she said.

"Thanks, Christine, it's a really good idea. We'll call the police on the way."

When we got to the Murphy's home, her father's car was parked in the driveway, and Tony had just parked his car, right behind it. We hadn't seen Orlando's car anywhere on the street.

"J.W.," Tony nodded.

"Hey, Tony, I didn't expect you to come here. I figured you'd just send a patrol car."

He ignored my comment, and asked a question. "Is this her father's car?"

I nodded.

"I'm going around into the back yard. Let me know the status," Tony said.

Christine and I went to the front door and rang the bell. I was sweating through my shirt. It was too hot to be wearing my sport coat, but I was required by law to cover up my handgun, when it was holstered. I had my Browning in my hand now.

The drapes moved and someone looked out at us. A moment later the door was opened by Larry Murphy.

"She's OK," he said. "There's been no sign of that little turd, so far. Come on in."

I introduced him to Christine, and called Tony on his cell phone. A moment later, Christine let him in through the back door. I introduced Tony to Mr. Murphy. Tony took the opportunity to speak up.

"Mr. Murphy, I pulled Orlando Cruz's criminal record. He has a history of violence. He's had several assault beefs, but he's slipped through the cracks. He did two years in juvenile detention on an armed robbery conviction. He's still on probation. We can pick him up if he shows up here. We can charge him with criminal mischief or making terroristic threats. That would violate his probation. If your daughter will testify against him, we can probably add kidnapping and sex trafficking to that. Do you think she'll cooperate?"

"I don't know. She's convinced he's more dangerous and determined than we understand. She says he's cruel and calculating. I think she's still too afraid of him. Lieutenant Escalante, she's a sixteen year old girl. I'm not going to put her through the embarrassment in open court."

"Where is she?" Christine asked.

"She's upstairs in her room, with the door locked."

"As long as she stays here, Orlando can show up at any time to grab her. I can't park a police officer here 24/7, on the mere possibility he might. Mr. Murphy, do you have family or friends she could stay with for a while?" Tony asked.

"He knows all her friends, and I don't like most of them as it is. I think they would tell Orlando where she is, if they knew. We don't have any family in this part of the country."

He looked at me.

"Mr. Tucker, can you arrange protection for her, here at the house?"

"Yes sir, I can, but it will get very expensive, very fast. This could go on for quite some time, until Orlando gives up and moves on to the next girl. He'll move on eventually, once he figures out the reward isn't worth the effort and the risk."

"She can stay with me," Christine said.

I was as startled by her statement, as her lack of hesitation.

"Christine, you don't know what you're saying. Having a sixteen year old girl staying with you, day and night, would not be a picnic. She might have to be with you for the rest of the summer. It would be better to send her to a distant relative." I suggested.

Christine looked thoughtful for a moment.

"Better for me maybe, but not better for her. If she's with me, I can make sure she doesn't have any contact with her friends, especially not with him. She won't have access to a cell phone or a computer, without me knowing about it. We'll be the only ones who know where she is. She'll be in our office during the day. If Orlando tries to make a move on us, we're better prepared to handle it. A distant relative could be caught unprepared."

"Well, I'll leave y'all to work out the details," Tony said.

When he got to the front door, Tony saw Mr. Murphy's camouflage Benelli Nova, twelve gauge shotgun, leaning against the wall by the door.

"Are you a bird hunter, Mr. Murphy?"

"Yes, I am, Lieutenant. I just hunt ducks and dove, mostly, quail and pheasant, when I can."

"Uh huh, I hunt too. This Benelli is a very good choice for wing shooting. It could also be a good home defense weapon. I see you're keeping it handy. The thing is, if you have to use it, you can't shoot someone in the street, in your yard, or on your porch. You can't use it unless they are an actual threat to you, in your own home. Do you understand what I'm saying?"

"Yes sir, I do."

"If your daughter stays here, he might do that. He might attack you in your own home. Can you really defend her with the shotgun, at any time of day or night? Do you think you could actually use it on a human being?"

Mr. Murphy thought about it for a moment.

"I don't want to have to find out." He stated honestly.

Tony nodded. "I'm sorry for your troubles. You called the right man. You follow Mr. Tucker's lead on this, and call me if you need my help."

Tony handed his card to Mr. Murphy. I walked out to his car with him.

We both saw the black SUV parked up the street.

"What do you plan to do about that?" Tony asked me, as he glanced in the direction of the SUV.

"… Nothing for now. They're just keeping track of me. Watching isn't illegal."

"No, but stalking is. You want me to go up there and rattle their cage, J.W.?"

"They already know I'm aware they're watching me. It might not hurt for them to know the police are aware of their activities as well."

Tony nodded. "Consider it done. How do you see Mr. Murphy's problem working out?"

"Orlando will go away, eventually, one way or another. Either he'll figure out Lori isn't available, or he'll do something stupid somewhere and end up in jail. I'll find a way to keep Lori safe, until he goes away. My challenge is to find a way to do it, without breaking Mr. Murphy financially in the process."

"Well, good luck with that."

"I don't believe in luck," I said.

Tony smiled.

"Yeah, I know."

"Why did you come over here, instead of just sending a patrol car, Tony?"

"Well, J.W., because I'm 'management' now, I'm tied to a desk most of the time. Whenever you call, I get to leave the desk, and I know whatever you're into, it will not be boring."

"You know me, Tony. I'm all about trying not to be a bore. Thanks again."

"Por nada, amigo." Tony replied.

When I went back into the house, Lori had come downstairs. She was sitting with her dad and Christine. They were chatting like they had known each other forever.

"John we've decided Lori should come stay with me for a while. It'll be fun, like having a little sister." She beamed at me.

"What about when you're working?"

"I'll bring her to work with me. We'll set her up in the work room with something fun to do or she can practice answering the phone."

"Lori, we probably ought to discuss this privately."

"No, John, we don't need to discuss it. Lori, tell him the plan."

Lori didn't look like she had been terrified less than an hour ago. She was smiling and seemed to think there was something funny about our conversation.

"Right, we'll hang out, watch movies and do girl stuff. I won't get in the way, I promise." She batted her eyes and tilted her head over to one side.

"Why?" I asked her.

"Why, what?" she asked in return.

"Why would you be interested in going to stay with a stranger?"

She looked at her dad.

"Everyone will be safer if Orlando doesn't know

where I am. He might try to find me here. But if I'm not here, he'll go away, right?"

She had been listening to our earlier conversation.

"It would seem to be the case. Typically, it is. But it only works if there is no way he can find you. You would have to promise not to expose your whereabouts to anyone other than your family. You wouldn't be able to see them very often, until we're sure he's done with you. You're going to find it isn't much fun. In fact it won't be any fun at all. We will never leave you alone. One of us will be with you at all times. Can you do that?"

"Oh, yes sir, I can. I promise."

I looked at Mr. Murphy.

"Sir, for security reasons, I can't even tell you where Christine lives. I'm sure you understand. I may have to move both of these ladies to an undisclosed location. Even if she does this, there's still a chance Orlando will come here looking for her. He might break into your house. I can suggest an alarm company."

"I have one coming this afternoon. We'll look after the home front, Mr. Tucker. Will you please keep my daughter safe?"

"Yes, sir, we'll get y'all through this."

"I'll arrange payment somehow. Will your daily rate be enough?"

"Mr. Murphy, my rate is five hundred dollars per day. That day rate is based on an eight hour day. We're providing protection for her effectively 24/7. That's thirty-five hundred dollars per week. This could go on for weeks. I know you make a good living, but you can't afford that. We'll have to give you the bulk buying discount."

"What's that?"

"I don't know. We'll work something out. We'll also find a way for y'all to spend some time together.

"Maybe we could meet at church?"

"Maybe, right now we'll be figuring it out as we go along. The situation is fluid. One day at a time."

CHAPTER 23

Christine helped Lori pack her things, ensuring there were no hidden cell phones or other communication devices making the trip.

When they were ready to go, I stepped outside and scanned the area. There was no sign of Orlando, but there was a huge scene going on up the street.

Tony had parked behind the subject SUV, with his lights flashing, and he had arranged for a couple of patrol cars to provide backup. The patrol cars had parked diagonally, obstructing the street at both ends of the block, with their blue and red lights flashing. People had come out of their homes to watch as the drama unfolded.

The two men who had been in the SUV were now sitting on the front lawn of someone's home, with a patrolman standing behind them. Tony and another uniformed officer were searching their vehicle.

"So much for being sneaky," I said.

Christine laughed.

This provided the perfect distraction for us to leave the area unobserved.

We drove straight to Christine's apartment to get Lori settled in. Christine's apartment was a two-bedroom unit. Christine's roommate had moved out a few months earlier and Christine liked having a "guest" room. Lori instantly fell in love with "Mr. Tumescence", Christine's cat. I could see that she and "Tummy" were going to become great friends.

Tony called me.

"I shook down those boys in the SUV."

"Yeah, I saw that. It was quite a scene. Why were you searching their vehicle?"

"They gave me permission. When I approached the vehicle, they were quick to show me their concealed carry permits. Both men were carrying Glock 19s. Get this - they had credentials for something called the 'World Wide Security Agency'. They had badges with WWSA worked into the logo. Badges, as if they were some sort of official agency! I was tempted to arrest them for imitating a Police Officer or Federal Agent. But they weren't actually doing that. It's more like they're 'rent-a-cops'. I explained to them we had received a report of a suspicious vehicle, and I asked if we could search their SUV. The bozos said 'yes', so we did."

"Did you find anything illegal?"

"No, J.W. Everything was very clean."

"Thanks, Tony. Maybe they'll get the message and leave me alone."

"There's something else, J.W."

"What's that?"

Christine was watching me closely.

"There were no wants or warrants out on either of them. They had no criminal records, and they were both former military."

"No surprise there."

"Ok, but neither of them was carrying their ID on their person. They had their wallets stashed in the console. They had to dig them out when I asked for their ID."

"Sounds sort of familiar, but it's not illegal, Tony."

"It sounds dangerous. Especially given that both of these guys sort of match the profile of the guy who tried to kill you a couple of months ago."

"Thanks, Tony. I hear what you're saying."

My research on the World Wide Security Agency turned up some rather interesting information. WWSA was a Private Security Contractor or PSC, often employed by various government agencies to provide security services for traveling diplomats and celebrities, in dangerous hot spots around the world.

I knew these guys. Not these guys in particular, but guys just like them. I had been detailed on missions where I had to work in close proximity with private contractors and Non-Government Organizations or NGOs.

In dangerous parts of the globe, in circumstances where use of the military would not be appropriate, various governments rely on PSCs to protect important assets and NGO employees. These PSCs are routinely manned by former military men, now making much better pay than they had made while working directly for Uncle Sam. I had nearly gone to work for one of those agencies myself. I probably would have, but the company got into some serious hot water when some civilians were killed in a controversial gun battle.

Further digging revealed the WWSA was owned by Strategic International Corporation, probably an umbrella corporation. I would have to do much more in depth research to find out who the real owners were.

What in the world did a PSC want with me? These guys and gals usually provided personal protection details for VIPs. Why would they be tailing me, and was there a connection to Simpson Oil and Gas Company?

At the office, Christine was schooling Lori on the proper etiquette for answering a business telephone.

"Good afternoon, Tucker Investigation, how may I direct your call?"

"That was really well done, girlfriend. You sounded professional and friendly, just perfect."

Christine gave Lori a little hug.

"Christine, can I see you in my office? Lori, you've got the phone. If anyone actually calls, you answer it just like that."

"Really, Mr. Tucker, can I answer the phone?"

"You bet, you keep working like you have been, we might just put you on the payroll. I think you should start calling me John, OK?"

Lori made a face. I realized my mistake.

"If it's OK with you, sir, I'll just call you Mr. Tucker or maybe 'Boss man'."

I nodded.

"That'll work."

When I had Christine in my office, behind closed doors, I opened a drawer in my desk and brought out a .380 semi-automatic handgun.

Christine raised her eyebrows, then her hands.

"I surrender," she said.

"Christine, do you have any experience shooting a handgun?"

She snorted.

How very unladylike!

"Are you kidding, I grew up in the Hill Country of Texas, with brothers. We all hunted and fished. I've fired pretty much all of the typically available handguns. Even toys like that one," she said, derisively.

"Guns aren't toys, Christine. I'm concerned for your safety."

She crossed her arms and looked at me, like I had just insulted her.

Today, Christine was wearing a grey skirt with a royal blue sleeveless blouse. Her hair was pulled back into a fancy, swirly thing behind her head. Her lipstick was red/orange, to match her hair. She had on silver jewelry.

She managed to look tough and beautiful, all at the same time.

"John, did you really think you were the only person around here that can shoot? I have a concealed carry permit. Right now, out there in my purse, I have a Lady Smith revolver in .357 magnum. That's my concealed carry piece. I prefer revolvers because they are highly reliable and always ready to fire. That little semi-auto gem has to be cocked, and it's subject to jamming. It's like a whittled down 9 mm."

I looked at her and put my hands up.

"I stand corrected."

"My daddy always told me, 'A lady should have a little something more about her than meets the eye.'"

"Well, you surely do, Christine."

She smiled.

"Count on it."

After Christine returned to the reception area, I called Tom Montgomery.

"Mr. Montgomery, I have concluded our investigation of Tim Shaw. We were unable to find anything to indicate that he is dangerous, or that he poses any sort of threat to you or your sister."

"Are you sure, I mean maybe there is something you could find out if you spent more time on surveillance."

"Yes, sir, I'm quite sure. There would be no point to any further surveillance."

"Yeah, well my information suggests you haven't followed him around enough, yet."

I thought about his statement.

... His 'information?' Now, who could have informed him of my surveillance endeavors?

"Mr. Montgomery, I've searched his background and current social and business activities. I've personally interviewed people who know him, and I've detailed one of my associates to do surveillance on him for several hours every day, for a week. I have video tape of him everywhere he's been after work, for the entire period of time. He's pretty much spent all his free time with your sister. I'm telling you there's nothing there. Your informant is wrong. If you'll tell me who your informant is, I'll interview him or her, and perhaps be able to gather more useful data."

"... Uhhh, no, that won't be necessary. I guess we're done then."

"Yes sir, we are done. I'll send you my bill."

"Ok fine... how much..."

"And please say 'hello' to Walter for me." I interrupted.

"Yeah, Ok, I mean... who's Walter?"

I hung up the phone.

This was starting to be fun.

CHAPTER 24

I saw Molly briefly that morning. She had just gotten back from re-hab.

"Hi, Johnny," she called.

"Hi yourself, Molly, you look terrific. What's going on?"

She was supervising men moving her things out of her apartment.

"I'm going home to Denver, Johnny. I can't stay here and get a fresh start. My folks want me to come home and live with them for a while."

I nodded. "Good for you, Molly. That sounds like a really good idea. Do they know what you're struggling with?"

"Yes, I told them everything. I want to thank you for all your help and support."

"Forget about it. I hope everything works out for you. Drop me a note or send me an e-mail sometime, just to let me know how you're doing."

She walked up to me and we hugged for a moment, very tight. Today there was no smell of alcohol seeping from her pores.

"I'm scared, Johnny," she whispered.

"Shoot! I'm not. You've got this. Go on and get it done."

She kissed me on the cheek, and then she gave

me a brave smile.

"You always did see the best in me."

"Now it's time for you to see it too. God don't make no junk, girl!"

"I know that's right," she grinned, and went back to her apartment.

Lori was sitting at Christine's desk, as Christine and I were in my office discussing what we had learned about Walter.

Lori buzzed me on the intercom.

"Hey, ya'll, there's somebody coming up the hall."

Lori was becoming a fixture at the office. She spent more and more time answering the phone, allowing Christine to make outgoing calls on her cell phone, and help me with research. Lori thought it was pretty cool, to be able to see people coming up the hall for their appointments, by watching the video monitor on the computer screen.

I didn't have any appointments scheduled for this time.

I clicked on the video feed to my computer screen.

The lady approaching the front door was very well dressed and appeared to be in her thirties. Christine went into the reception area to meet her.

I switched cameras, so my monitor showed the view from just behind Lori's head.

The lady was about Christine's height, maybe five feet, three inches, but more like 5'6", in her high heels. She had medium length, blonde hair and appeared to me to be quite pretty, elegant and poised, as she greeted Christine and Lori.

Presently, there was a knock on my door, and Christine brought the lady into my office.

"John, this is Melody Doyle, of Doyle, Doyle and

Starnes. Ms. Doyle, this is Mr. Tucker."

"Please call me John," I said, as I shook her hand.

I was amused to see Christine take a seat in one of the upholstered chairs in front of my desk, at the same time Ms. Doyle did.

I knew Doyle, Doyle and Starnes, was one of the law firms in this building, located just down the hall, on this floor.

"Is this a neighborly visit, or do we have business to discuss?"

"A little bit of both, I reckon." She said, with a grin. "I've been curious about ya'll, since I saw you moving in. When they put the plaque up 'Tucker Investigation,' I got even more curious."

"Well then, Ms. Doyle, welcome to Tucker Investigation. How may we be of service?"

Christine was watching all this with amusement.

"Melody, John, please call me Melody. I'll get right to the point. Doyle, Doyle and Starnes, our law firm, specializes in both criminal defense, and personal injury. The other Doyle is my dad, Clarence Doyle the Third. Jeff Starnes is the remaining partner. We have need of an investigator to provide information related to our client's cases."

I appreciated how direct she was. I like people who get right to the point.

"I see. I'm surprised you don't have an investigator already."

"We did, until yesterday. It seems our investigator may have a serious drug problem. We put up with it for as long as we could. He managed to get himself arrested again yesterday, so we fired him. Now he's one of our clients!"

"Melody, you wouldn't hire another investigator without checking out references, would you?"

She smiled, real big. My, what pearly white teeth she had!

"No, John, we wouldn't. Of course we followed the story of the rescue of those girls back in the spring, never imagining you would be moving into this building. That was a very nice piece of work, by the way. When we heard our investigator had been arrested again, I made a few phone calls. You check out fine."

I thought I saw Christine narrow her eyes at Ms. Doyle's last comment.

"We would be delighted to be of service from time to time, Melody, but because of our client list, I'm not in a position to go to work for your firm, exclusively."

"Oh, we're not asking you to work exclusively for us. We can probably keep ya'll pretty busy though. How many investigators do you have?"

"Christine and I are the only full-time employees. We have other people who do work for us on a part time, contract basis, and we have arrangements with some other agencies."

Melody looked back and forth between Christine and me.

"Oh, I see. Well, that sounds just fine. Perhaps you could come down to our office to meet with the other partners and discuss the details."

"Yes, I'll be happy to do so. Christine will work out an appointment time," I said, standing up.

After Melody was gone, Christine came back into my office and sat down.

"Thank you, John."

"Thank you, for what?"

"Whenever you talk about Tucker Investigation, you always say 'we,' including me in the equation. It means a lot to me. I'm afraid you gave Melody the wrong impression though."

"... How's that?"

She rolled her eyes.

"John, you are as dense as a brick! She thinks we are a couple. She was flirting with you, and you made her think we're a couple."

"Yeah, she was coming on a little too strong and fast for me. Besides, you are the only woman in my life." I winked.

"You do know you and I are not ever going to be romantically linked, right?"

Yeah, I knew that. I had always known we weren't destined to be a couple. It's very difficult for Shepherds to have wives. We tend to out-live them. Shepherds have the same desires as other people walking around in earth-suits, but my mission cannot be jeopardized by my personal desires. Our one and only date had been delightful, but there was never going to be a second date. We were good together, just not romantically good. We flirted occasionally, but we both knew it was never really going anywhere.

"Right, I get it. I mean we only ever had one real date, right?"

She smiled, a bit wistfully.

"John, we couldn't work together if I thought you were trying to get me into bed."

"Good grief, Christine you didn't think I was trying to do that, did you?"

She squinted and made a face.

"No, John, of course not, you haven't done anything of the kind. That would be Walter's way of doing business."

As I was heading home, I saw Dustin pushing his shopping cart down the sidewalk, so I decided to stop and see how he was doing. The temperature was hovering at about a hundred and one degrees, and Dustin was wearing a hooded sweatshirt.

"Hello, good Angel," he grinned.

"Hi, Dustin," I grinned back. "Man, it's too hot out here. You need to find a cool spot somewhere. Can I take you to a place with some air conditioning?"

"The day is hot, but I is cool. The one who's your

shadow, be a fool."

"Oh boy, here we go." I thought.

"Well, it's kind of shady right here, but it doesn't help much with the heat."

"You got a long dark shadow following you, Angel."

Was he referring to the black SUV? Could he have seen it following me?

"This time of day we all have long shadows."

"This kinda shadow hate the light, he try to hurt you, with all his might."

What the…? I thought.

"You got to keep on keepin' on, Angel."

"We all do Dustin, even you, right?"

"Nah suh, I'm wrong in the head, and it's not my fight."

"Are you sure I can't get you a motel room or take you somewhere cooler?

He smiled kind of a sad smile, and started pushing his cart.

"I got me my rounds, and, ain't nobody cooler'n me."

"Well, OK Dustin, drink lots of water."

He started pushing his cart away, indicating our conversation was over. He looked back over his shoulder and said, "You watch your back, good Angel. Shadows don't come at you straight on."

CHAPTER 25

The very next day, Walter Farley came by to see us.

I was sitting at my desk, when Lori buzzed me. Christine had gone to the restroom.

"Mr. Tucker, there's someone here to see you."

Lori was kind of laughing, as she said it.

I clicked over to the video feed from behind her head.

There stood Walter, all grins, as he chatted with Lori.

"Send him in, Lori."

A moment later, Walter Farley sauntered into my office.

"Whooee boy, you've come up in the world!"

"Hello, Walter. What can I do for you?"

"Not what you can do for me, but what I can do for you."

"Have a seat, Walter."

"No thanks, I'll stand. Where's Christine? You didn't have to fire her too, did you? She's a tease, but she won't put out. Now, the little cutie you have out front is a nice touch, but she seems a little young for you."

I couldn't sit there with Walter standing in front of me, looking down on me.

"OK, Walter, you can sit down, or get out."

"Whoa there, pardner, this is a friendly visit. I don't mind sitting."

While Walter was sitting down, I glanced at the monitor. Christine was back, casually talking to Lori at the desk.

"You know, Walter, the last time you were sitting in my office, you left a bug under the chair. I hope you don't try the same, lame trick, again."

"Golly, Mr. Tucker, for a busy and popular guy, you sure are grouchy. What's the matter, not getting any?"

"You have ten seconds to get to the point, Walter, eight now, when I get to one, I'm going to throw you out. You've got three seconds now."

He held up his hands.

"OK, OK! I've called off my watch dogs. That's the point. I just wanted you to know I'm not having them follow you anymore."

"What, exactly, was the purpose of that, in the first place?"

"I just wanted you to know what real surveillance feels like. I wanted you to see what resources I have at my disposal. You're supposed to be this big shot security expert. I figured you might enjoy seeing real professionals in action."

I looked him in the eye. There was nothing there. It was like looking into a lizard's eyes. No, a lizard has more soul. Looking into his eyes, was like looking down, into an empty well, a deep, deep, well, containing nothing but emptiness, entombed in darkness.

"I'd have to say, I'm not impressed."

He looked... disappointed.

"John, I have personal control over nearly two hundred security agents."

"The one's I've seen so far might make pretty fair school crossing guards, but that's about all they're good for."

"Well, John, if you'd done your homework, you

would have learned I personally founded the World Wide Security Agency, but, you're not that good a detective are you?

I shrugged. "Maybe not, but once I learned you were the CEO of Strategic International Corporation, I got distracted. I decided to look into your life a little deeper. Why are you working as Mr. Simpson's personal assistant?"

Walter looked startled for a second, and then anger clouded his features.

"Oh, John, you've surely put your foot in it now. I came to give you the chance to bow out gracefully, without getting hurt. I may have to re-think my position." He growled.

"Leave now, Walter, or I can promise you won't like where I put my foot."

He showed his teeth in a snarl, which might have been mistaken for a smile.

"Yes, of course, if that's the way you feel about it. Well then until we meet again…" He stood up and pointed his finger at me, as though it were a gun. "I'll be seeing you." He dropped his thumb.

I got up and followed him out the door into the reception area. Christine went white as a sheet, when she saw him coming out of my office.

Walter looked over at Lori and waved. "Bye, bye, cutie pie," he winked.

"Oh, there you are, Christine! It looks like old John here has better taste in women than I thought. See you around."

When he had left, Christine and I went back into my office to talk.

"What was he doing here?" Christine asked.

I sighed.

"I'm not sure. At first it was as if he were gloating about how smart and powerful he thinks he is. When he left, he was sort of threatening."

"Why? What's all this about?"

I shook my head. "I think, in his mind, he's playing some sort of game with me. I don't get it. I think I know what motivates him, but I don't know why this is personal for him."

We both sat and thought about Walter Farley for a while.

"What do I have to do to get that tongue flicking snake out of my life?" Christine asked.

"Christine, I don't think this is about you. I don't think he's capable of really caring about anyone, but himself."

"You've got that right," she said.

I looked at the monitor. Lori was talking to someone on the phone. I saw her laugh.

I got the call at about 9:30 that night.

"Well, Mr. Tucker, you were right, he showed up. He rang the front door bell, and caught me flat footed. I opened the front door and there he was, big as life."

"Mr. Murphy, are you saying Orlando Cruz was there, at your house? Are you and your wife OK?"

"Yes, we're pretty shaken up, but we're OK. I just didn't think he would walk right up to the front door and ring the bell. It was as if he just showed up there to pick up his date, or deliver a pizza, or something."

"Then what happened?"

"He saw me look at my shotgun as I was trying to shut the door, but he slammed his body into the door, and it knocked me off balance. The next thing I knew he was standing in our foyer, holding my shotgun."

I closed my eyes, and took a long slow breath.

"He pointed the gun at my wife and told me to call Lori downstairs. I told him Lori wasn't home, that we had sent her away. He didn't believe me, so he forced us to go upstairs to Lori's room. It was obvious she hadn't been there for some time."

"OK, did you call the police?"

"Yes, they're here now. They're going through the house, the yard and the neighborhood, to be sure he's not here anymore, but he's long gone."

"Did Orlando ask you where she was?"

"Yes, but I lied. I told him Lori had showed up on our doorstep, looking like a tramp, and we had told her to go away. I told him we had no idea where she went. He believed me. That's when it got scary."

"… In what way?"

"We could see he didn't know what to do next. He was holding the shotgun, and I think he wanted to shoot us. I'm not sure he knew how to work a semi-auto shotgun, because he never took the safety off. He finally just took off running down the stairs and out the front door. He took the shotgun with him."

"He's in deep grease now. He's guilty of breaking and entering, robbery and use of a firearm in a crime, among other things. He's on the run, and he's armed and presumed dangerous. The cops are going to want him, real bad."

"That's what they said. Your friend Lieutenant Escalante is here, he'd like to speak to you."

"Put him on."

"J.W., these folks are safe, and 'lover boy' is on the run. You might want to stay vigilant for a few more days, but I think this deal is over. We've got an APB out on him; he won't be able to run for long, before somebody catches him. Until then, he'll run like a scalded cat."

"Thanks, Tony. Let me talk to Mr. Murphy again."

"Mr. Murphy, I just wanted you to know Lori is safe with my partner Christine. I'll let Christine know what's happened. We'll talk again tomorrow. You folks try to relax. You've done very well under the circumstances. I'm terribly sorry Orlando showed up, and that he broke into your house, but, again, you handled it as best you could. You can thank God, you and your wife are still alive. All is well. Good night."

"Thank you, Mr. Tucker. Good night."

I called Christine and gave her the news. She said she thought we ought to wait till morning to tell Lori.

We didn't get to wait until the morning. Lori was watching TV. The story about the home invasion, the invasion of her family's home, was on the ten o'clock news.

CHAPTER 26

When Christine brought Lori into the office the next morning, they were both subdued.

I still haven't learned to ignore women's moods, so I asked.

"Good morning ladies, why the long faces?"

As usual, wrong question and bad timing.

"You should mind your own business," Christine snapped.

Ouch, I thought I was minding my own business. Think again.

"OK, is now a good time for us to talk about planning for Lori's return to her family. Lori, school starts in a few weeks, and I've been talking to your mom and dad about that…"

"No, John now is not the time to be discussing this," Christine interrupted, between tightly clenched teeth.

"Right, sorry, I'll just be in my office if you need me."

I retreated, with some haste. After all, I'm easily frightened.

I was reading the story in the Tyler paper, about the home invasion in a south Tyler neighborhood, when Christine came in.

"John, I'm sorry I snapped at you. We stayed up pretty late last night, and Lori and I have been arguing this morning."

I waited.

"Lori's not sure she wants to go home, or go back to school. After the story on the news last night, she was pretty upset. We sat up and talked about a lot of things. At first it was about how unhappy she was because she had endangered her parents. Then, she talked about how horrible Orlando is, but how he still has some pull on her. She's been through a lot, John, and she doesn't feel like a typical high school girl."

"I understand."

"No, John, you don't. You've never been a teenage girl, and you've never been through what she's been through."

I nodded.

"… Fair enough."

"Lori doesn't want to have to face her friends, and she's afraid Orlando could still find her. She feels like she's more grown up than she actually is. She wants to get her own place and continue to work here."

"Is that what you were arguing about?" I checked the monitor, which was still showing the view from the camera in the reception area. It looked like Lori was talking on the phone.

"No, we were arguing about Walter."

"Walter…?"

"She thought he was cute and charming. I told her he was a dangerous jackass. I offended her, and I made her feel little, and… I think I hurt her feelings."

"She'll get over it."

Christine was thoughtful for a moment.

"Anyway," I said, "She has to go home. She has to go back to school, and she can't continue to work here."

"Maybe we could work something out. At least

until we know Orlando Cruz can't come after her. She really can't go home, until he's in jail."

She had a point.

"OK, that part hasn't changed. If you're still willing to have her stay with you, we'll keep her with us, until Orlando is in jail. I've been talking with her folks about school. They want to put her into a private school. It could be a new beginning. She'd make new friends and be in a safer environment."

Christine smiled.

"It's perfect. I'll tell her about it."

"Wait, there's more. Her folks are thinking about the possibility of moving away from Tyler altogether, maybe to Houston or Austin. They'll need to be the ones to talk about those things with Lori."

Christine nodded.

"Probably even better, it really would be a new beginning."

"Sometimes, we all need a new beginning. The bible says when we are born again, old things are washed away and we are new creations, spiritually re-born as children of God, and no longer slaves to sin."

"Here we go again!"

"What? I'm just saying Lori has a new life. Is she still reading her bible?"

Christine sighed.

"Yes, she reads it every morning, for all the good it will do her."

"Do you read it?"

"No, John I don't. I wouldn't even know where to start. It's just a lot of poetry and superstitious blah, blah, blah."

"And, you know this without ever having read it? You are able to stand on the platform of complete ignorance and deride something you know nothing about?"

She made an annoyed snort. It sounded sort of like "Humph!"

"If you're willing to at least look at it, I'll suggest some places to start, and I would love to discuss it with you. You're a bright, intelligent and literate person. What are you afraid of?"

"Nothing, it just seems pointless."

"What harm could it do?"

"It could turn me into a right wing, brainwashed, hypocritical, zombie."

"Is that what you think I am?"

She looked me in the eye.

"No, John, I'm sorry, it just came out wrong."

"Christine, I love you… Relax, I'm not hitting on you. The point is you must know I love you, as a friend and colleague. I have no desire to ever see you hurt or 'brainwashed'. Do you believe me?"

She hesitated.

There it was. She had doubts.

"Yes, John, I know you aren't trying to brainwash me. I'm just not interested in reading the bible."

"No worries. It was just a thought."

"How did we get on this subject in the first place?"

"We were talking about new beginnings."

"We were talking about Lori."

I nodded.

"So, are you two ladies going to work it out?"

"Of course, but let's hope Orlando goes away soon, and I mean very soon."

"Amen, to that."

CHAPTER 27

Orlando Cruz was stopped for a traffic violation in College Station. Once identified, he was arrested on the spot, but not without a struggle. He attacked one of the arresting officers with a knife. A search of his car revealed he was in possession of the stolen shotgun, and several controlled substances. Eventually, as the wheels of justice turned their course, he would be returned to Tyler to stand trial on the home invasion and theft charges.

As soon as we learned of his arrest, we had a little celebration in honor of the occasion, at "Currants" restaurant. Mr. Murphy hosted the event.

"I'd like to propose a toast." He waited for us all to raise our glassware. "Here's to our daughter, Lori, as strong and courageous a person as I've ever met, we love you, honey!" We all bumped glasses and bottles.

Lori was beaming.

"And, here's to the fine work of the police, in catching that… suspect," I added, gesturing toward Tony.

Tony bowed slightly, willing to take the credit due all policemen, everywhere.

"Hear, hear!" everyone said.

"How long do you think he'll be in prison?" Lori asked.

Tony considered the various possibilities.

"Well, first there's the issue of his Probation violation. He'll have to serve out the full term for the previous crime. Then there's the drug possession charges, he's looking at two to five years on that. Possession of stolen property, breaking and entering, two counts of assault with a deadly weapon, assault on a police officer, use of a firearm in a criminal act, resisting arrest... he'll be sentenced to a minimum of 25 years, I would guess, maybe a lot more, depending on the jury."

"Do you think the judge might probate his sentence?" Mrs. Murphy asked.

Tony shook his head.

"No, there's no chance. His lawyers will tell Orlando to make a deal with the DA, though."

"What does that mean?" Lori asked.

"They'll tell Orlando to plead guilty to some of the charges, in exchange for the District Attorney dropping or reducing some of the other charges. That's why he'll only get 25 years or so. Otherwise, the sky's the limit. He could spend several decades in prison."

"Isn't it possible he could get out early?" Mr. Murphy asked.

"Yes, with good behavior, his sentence could be cut in half. He'd be out in about twelve years. But Orlando doesn't strike me as the model prisoner type."

"What about bail?" Mr. Murphy asked.

"I don't know who'd bail him out. He has no family. Because of the nature of his crimes, his bail will be set high, at least a hundred thousand dollars, probably more. After they transfer him back here, he'll sit in the Smith County Jail, for months, waiting on his trial. Then, it will be off to the big house."

"I'll drink to that." Mrs. Murphy said.

I thought about the thing we weren't discussing. Lori would not have to testify in open court. Because Orlando wouldn't face any charges related to what he had done with and to Lori, she would never have to appear in court at all.

I smiled to myself, but evidently Christine saw it.

"You look kind of smug, John. Shouldn't a religious person like you want mercy for Orlando?"

"I'm not his judge, Christine. I'm just happy Lori won't have to testify in court."

"Oh, right, I see your point. How wonderful!"

She smiled too. She held up her hand for a "high five."

"I saw that, Christine!" Lori said. "You're just happy you'll be able to have me out of your apartment."

"No," Christine said. "We're just happy you're safe from that bum."

"As are we all, honey," Lori's father added.

"We're very grateful to you for all the two of you have done for Lori and us. You went over and above any service we could possibly have hoped for." Mrs. Murphy said.

Christine and I looked at each other.

"It has been our pleasure," we said, in unison.

Everybody laughed.

"I'm afraid there is still the issue of payment." I said.

It would have been a wholly inappropriate time to mention it, but...

"... It seems to me Lori will have to spend the rest of the summer in our office, working off her portion of our fee."

Lori's face lit up!

"Can I, please?" she asked her folks.

Her dad smiled.

"Well, I only see one complication with that..."

"What, can't we figure out some sort of car pool

arrangement?" Lori asked.

Her father grinned.

"That's the complication. If you're going to go through driver's education, you'll have to figure out how to fit it into your schedule."

"Oh, yeah, I nearly forgot, I can get my driver's license now!"

We discussed various ways to solve the scheduling crisis.

Then Lori's father brought up a new topic.

"We want ya'll to know our plans. We've discussed it as a family, and we're not moving away from Tyler. We're not giving up the life we've made here, because of this time of trouble we've had. Lori will start back at high school in the fall, at a private school. By this time next year, she'll be looking forward to her senior year."

We all applauded.

Redemption is cool.

CHAPTER 28

I asked Christine how often she practiced with her handgun. She indicated she only shot two or three times a year, probably even less often. In my experience, more is better, so I invited her to come along the next time Tony and I were scheduled to shoot.

"As often as we've been coming here, if I had known I could have been shooting with Christine, instead of you..." Tony said.

Christine laughed.

"You don't say? Well, today's your lucky day."

Christine shot her .357. She was using .38 ammo, to reduce the recoil and muzzle lift, shooting very well at ten feet, poorly at ten yards, and hit or miss beyond that.

"Most gun fights happen within about twenty feet," Tony said. "You shoot well enough at that distance here on the shooting range, but in a desperate situation, with your adrenaline pumping, your hands might shake, your breathing might change, the lighting might be bad, etc. You need to practice more, so that shooting feels natural to you and you're completely comfortable with your weapon."

"You're a police officer, Tony. Have you ever had

to shoot someone?"

Tony glanced at me.

"Not since I've been a detective. I've had my weapon drawn several times since then, but I didn't have to fire it. When I was a rookie patrol officer, my training officer and I had to apprehend a suspect in an apartment. I was the first one in, and the suspect grabbed a handgun as I came through the door. He started firing as he ducked behind a half-wall in the kitchen, and I started firing, as I dived behind the end of his sofa. We were only about ten feet apart. We both emptied our guns at each other, but neither of us was hit. We were both too scared to look at each other, or take the time to aim. When the shooting stopped, my training officer came in and made the arrest."

"That's my point. It seems like John and you are always carrying your guns, but never using them. You're telling me the one time you did have to shoot it, you missed. What's the point really?"

Tony looked at me again, then back at Christine.

"Christine if I had gone into that apartment without the gun. He would have shot me for sure. I was a rookie; I had barely qualified with my revolver, on the range, and before that incident, I had never had it out of the holster, on the job. I am much more experienced and proficient now. Which underscores my point, training and practice is extremely important."

"OK, fine, but you're a cop. You have to be ready to defend yourself. I just like to shoot, I don't really know if I could actually shoot someone."

"If you don't train, and you aren't capable of actually using it to defend yourself, or someone else, you're a sportsman with rudimentary skills. That's fine; it's a fairly inexpensive hobby."

Tony shrugged, and looked over at me, raising his eyebrows

"Christine, the world is a dangerous place. Here

in America; most people are safe, most of the time. If you feel safe, you probably are safe. Tony and I choose to put ourselves in harm's way, so the probability of a violent altercation is increased for us. The thing you don't seem to know is when something really bad happens, typically, the police don't show up until after the shooting stops. When seconds count, the police are only a few minutes away. The police are seldom able to prevent a violent crime; mostly they clean up after the crime. Tony, correct me if I'm wrong."

"J.W. is right, Christine. As police officers, we usually respond to the scene of a violent crime, we seldom get to prevent them, and like you mentioned earlier, cops carry guns so we can protect ourselves. We don't carry them for your protection."

Christine was thoughtful for a moment, and then Tony spoke up again.

"You know the story of how J.W. saved my life, right? Well, if he hadn't been carrying his .45, Whitaker would have blown my head off with his twelve-gauge shotgun. I also know Whitaker must have looked J.W. in the eye, and known he wouldn't hesitate to use his .45. Otherwise, he would have shot J.W. with the shotgun. Would you have shot him, J.W.?"

They both looked at me.

I nodded. "When I thought he had probably killed Tony, I wanted to shoot him. If he had so much as blinked wrong... You'll also remember Mr. Murphy had a shotgun handy when Orlando forced his way into their home, but Mr. Murphy didn't know how or when to use it in a dangerous situation. It was less useful to him than a banana would have been."

She nodded and said, "Orlando could have killed both of them with Mr. Murphy's own gun."

Tony looked at Christine.

"You were protecting Lori at that point. What

would you have done if Orlando broke into your apartment?"

Christine nodded.

"OK, I need more training."

Tony and I looked at each other.

"First, and this is essential; Do everything you can to avoid situations where shooting is the only way to stay alive. Run away from trouble, every time, if you can. However, if it comes down to it, there are some fundamental things you need to understand. Let's start with some basic concepts," Tony said. "Let's think about what a gun does. It fires a projectile…

… She had a .357, just like you, and just like you, she figured it was a better choice for firepower. Even though she was a trained police officer, she didn't want to kill the intruder, so after she threatened to shoot him, and he continued to approach her, she shot him in the right leg, about six inches above the knee. That stopped him, for a second, and then it made him mad. He rushed at her and they wrestled around for control of the gun. She managed to shoot him two more times, flesh wounds, but he punched her in the face, knocking her out, breaking some facial bones. She could have been raped or murdered at that point. Because he was wounded, he fled her home and was arrested about forty minutes later at a hospital. He was eventually convicted on multiple rape charges, from previous assaults." Tony paused for a moment.

"The point is this, shot placement is far more important than what caliber you shoot. She had five .357 hollow points, and she shot him three times. She didn't stop him. It barely slowed him down. He was able to attack her. She was seriously injured and he could have killed her," Tony concluded.

"She had five rounds of .357 hollow points, more than enough to do the job. One would have been enough, if she had put it where it needed to go. Now, some people rely on more bullets, as if having 13, or 15, or 18 bullets is better than one correct shot. It's all about stopping the antagonist. One bullet in the right place will get the job done. You aim for center mass, because the heart, lungs, all the vital organs and major vascular structures are there. You aim for the heart and shoot till the subject falls. The purpose of deadly force is to stop the attacker. Once he falls, stop shooting. That's when you get to safety and get help." I said.

Tony nodded. "You aren't out to kill someone, Christine, but you can't hope to shoot the gun out of their hand either. You have to stop them. If they don't survive the altercation... Dead people don't shoot you and they don't sue you," he added.

Christine looked shocked.

"I don't know if I could do that. How can you choose to end someone's life? It makes you the judge, jury and executioner.

"No," Tony said, "it makes you the survivor. If you're alive, you can handle the aftermath and the associated legal issues and still be with your family. Dead is dead."

I nodded my agreement. "Christine, everyone dies. How a person dies is not as important as how a person lives. All people die, and no matter how they die, they go on to face their final judgment. They do have a Judge, but it isn't you."

"Why can't we all just get along? Sometimes, I wish all the guns were gone," she said.

I shrugged, and said, "Then I'd have to go back to carrying a sword. It's hard to get in and out of a car or truck, with one of those things hanging off your belt,"

Christine laughed, probably at the mental picture.

The next day, I read in the paper that our old friend, Orlando Cruz was expected to be transferred to the Smith County jail, to await trial in Tyler on the home invasion and associated charges

CHAPTER 29

I love autumn in East Texas. In the fall, the leaves change color, hunting season opens, the holidays are approaching, and we anticipate a fire in the fireplace.

In the fall, the Rose City, hosts the Tyler Rose Festival which brings people from all over the country to participate in the festival, see our spectacular Rose garden, and enjoy the city. But the thing I love best is the change in the weather. Summer's heat is finally broken.

Lori had started a new school year, at a new school, with a newish car. She was living the life of a typical American teenager. Because I was tied up with the trial of Evan Whitaker, Christine was handling the whole operation. We had people doing the skip tracing, subject surveillance, and other investigative activities, while Christine managed the office and did research.

I was testifying in Federal Court as a witness in the Whitaker trial.

"So, you're saying you were able to identify Mr. Whitaker's car, based on a tip from an anonymous person. Is that correct?

"The person I spoke to indicated on the day Victoria Winslow was abducted, he had seen a man strike a female child and put her into the trunk of a blue, or possibly black, Chevrolet Impala. He said he saw this occur in a parking lot, just down the street from the supermarket where Victoria Winslow was last seen. He wrote down the license number of the vehicle on a scrap of paper, but he was unable to find the scrap of paper for several days."

"Did you inform the police about this anonymous tip?"

"Yes, I did."

"Specifically, who did you speak to?"

"I spoke to Detective Sergeant Anthony Escalante, who was working the case at that time."

"Detective Sergeant Anthony Escalante, now Lieutenant Anthony Escalante, of the Tyler Police Department, is that correct?"

"Yes, it is."

"What was his response to the information you provided him."

"He informed me the FBI had identified the suspect vehicle as possibly being a Chevrolet Impala."

"What did he do about the information you gave him?"

"I don't know. You'll have to ask him."

The defense attorney was thoughtful for a beat.

"Let's go back to this tip from this 'anonymous' person, for a moment. How did this 'anonymous' person contact you?" He was emphasizing the word, by indicating quotation marks with his fingers.

"I don't understand the question. Are you asking me how he knew I had been hired by the Winslows, to try to find their daughter?"

"Uhhhh, yes, how did he know that?"

"I don't know. I have no reason to think he did."

"… Objection your honor! What is the point of this questioning? How an anonymous person knew who to contact is irrelevant," the prosecuting attorney interjected.

"I'll prove the relevance in just a moment, Your Honor."

"Very well, I'll permit this line of questioning to continue for a moment, but get to the point quickly, Counsellor. Objection overruled," said the judge.

"Now then, Mr. Tucker isn't it true you actually know the person who provided you with this tip. Isn't it true you met with him face to face?"

"Which question do you want me to answer first?" I asked the judge.

"When you ask a question, Counselor, ask just one question at a time and one question only. Is that understood?" the judge directed.

"Yes, Your Honor." The defense attorney replied. He changed the question.

"Mr. Tucker, do you know the person who gave you the tip?"

"At the time he first told me what he had seen…"

"Yes, or no, Mr. Tucker, do you know the person who gave you the tip?"

"Yes, I do. No, I didn't. This is not a question that can be answered with a simple 'yes' or 'no.'"

"… Permission to treat the witness, as a hostile witness, Your Honor?"

"I want to hear what Mr. Tucker has to say. The witness is directed to answer the question, in his own words. Take your time, Mr. Tucker," the judge ruled.

"Thank you, Your Honor. I had no idea who the man who gave me the initial tip was, at the time he gave it to me. In that sense, he was an anonymous person. I immediately contacted Detective Sergeant Escalante and told him about our conversation. He informed me the man I had spoken to was a person that was known to the police. They had questioned him at the time of the abduction and had ruled him out as a suspect. He is a homeless man with limited mental capacity. The information he gave me has proven to be accurate."

"So, you do know him, and he is not an 'anonymous' person. Isn't that true?"

"... Objection. Asked and answered, Your Honor!" The prosecutor interjected.

"Objection sustained. Move on, Counselor. Redirect your line of questioning." The judge ordered.

The defense attorney took it in stride.

"When did you first learn the name of the man who is now accused of these crimes?"

"At the time we found him with the abducted girls."

"How did you learn his name?"

"Lieutenant Escalante told me."

"How did Lieutenant Escalante determine my client was a suspect in these crimes?"

"You'll have to ask him that question."

"Surely, he told you something."

"... Objection! Your Honor, this is not a question the witness can answer." The prosecutor interjected.

"Withdrawn, Your Honor I'll rephrase my question."

That was the way my day was going. We had discussed with the prosecutor how we ought to handle the issue with Dustin. He said the defense had little going for them, except to discredit Dustin as a reliable source of information. Of course it wouldn't ultimately do them any good. Their client was captured with the girls in his trailer. He had confessed to the crimes at the time of his capture, and there was an overwhelming amount of physical and forensic evidence gathered from his car and his trailer in the woods. The evidence alone was enough to get a conviction. The girls had been interviewed on video tape under the supervision of their guardians and mental health professionals. These video interviews would be the only testimony introduced from the victims. They would not be asked to appear in open court. Other professionals would describe the mental, physical and emotional effects on the girls, sustained during their abductions and their treatment by Whitaker.

The prosecutor had met with the defense attorneys to ensure Dustin wouldn't have to testify. The defense was pretty focused on trying to make Tony and I look bad.

I knew the defense team was doing all they could, but there was no real defense for Whitaker. He had been found mentally competent, and a finding of insanity would have been their only hope.

Their defense was so pointless it looked to me like they were almost trying to do so poorly their client might later win an appeal, based on the incompetency of their defense.

By the time the judge adjourned the trial for the night, I was dead tired. I stumbled out of the courthouse with only one desire, to go in search of a big, thick steak. On my way to the truck, I remembered to turn my cell phone back on. There were several messages. I listened to the one from Christine.

"John, call me as soon as you get this message."

I did.

"Hey, Christine, what's going on?"

"You are not going to believe this. Lori has been talking to Walter. They're even friends on Facebook."

I thought about all the possible implications of this new wrinkle.

"John, did you hear me?"

"Yes, I did, I was just considering how to respond."

"… How to respond? For crying out loud, we've got to put a stop to this!"

"Right… I understand how you feel, but what exactly do you plan to do?"

"What do I plan to do? What do you plan to do?"

"Christine, can we talk about this tomorrow? I've spent the whole day giving testimony in the Whitaker trial, and I don't know up from down at this point."

She was quiet for a moment. I could feel her beginning to calm down.

"I'm sorry. How's the trial going?"

"Well they're done with me for now, though I'll probably be called back later. The defense is trying really hard to discredit everything about the case, the evidence, my involvement, Tony, Dustin, everything."

"Can they do that? Are they winning?"

"They can try to, they have to try, and no, they aren't winning. They can't win; the State has a lock on this."

"But all they have to do is get the jury to think there is a possibility Whitaker is innocent…" She observed

"There's no chance of that, Christine, but they have to try everything they possibly can."

"OK, so we're winning?"

"Yeah, we're winning, but it sure is a struggle."

CHAPTER 30

When I finally returned to the office, Christine sent a call through on line one.

"Hello, John Tucker, speaking."

"Mr. Tucker, my name is Edward Nordstrom. I'll get straight to the point. I work for WWSA. Does that ring a bell?"

The World Wide Security Agency, yes, it rang a bell alright. Was Edward Nordstrom one of Walter Farley's goons?

"Yes, Mr. Nordstrom, I'm familiar with the WWSA. A little too familiar for my tastes, what can I do for you."

"Well, to be brief, I need a job. Now, don't hang up on me. Please hear me out."

"I'm listening."

"I can't continue to work for WWSA. I can't work for Farley anymore. The guy is nuts. He's not paying on time, and he's obsessed with you, for some reason."

"I'm aware of those things. You have to be aware me hiring you, would be pretty stupid on my part, considering the fact Walter Farley is apparently out to get me."

"Yes, sir, I thought you would see it that way. I'd like to sit down with you and explain the situation, as I see it. There is something about the relationship between Walter Farley and Ted Simpson you don't know. If you won't hire me, I'll completely understand."

"Will you come to my office?"

"Yes sir, when would you like me to be there?"

"Tomorrow evening, at 1800."

"I'll arrange it. Thank you."

"One more thing, Mr. Nordstrom... Make real sure you come alone, come unarmed, and be prepared to answer some tough questions."

"Yes sir."

Christine came into my office.

"Is now a good time for us to talk about Lori?"

I pointed to one of the richly upholstered chairs.

"John, we have to do something. We can't let her go on having a relationship with Walter."

"How do you know she is friendly with Walter?"

"She told me. We talk two or three times a week and we text back and forth. We're friends on Facebook. That's where I saw Walter pop up."

"Have you talked to her folks?"

"Not yet, I wanted to talk to you first. We need to come up with a plan."

There was a lot to consider.

"Here's the thing Christine. She isn't our responsibility anymore...."

I held up my hand, as she started to interrupt.

"... Knowing Walter, like we do, there's a probability he's planning to use Lori to get at us in some way. I get that. We'll talk to her parents and tell them we think Walter is dangerous, and they should try to end Lori's friendship with him."

"I don't care about Walter's plans. I just don't want Lori to get hurt by that jerk."

"Right, but she's their daughter. We'll let them deal with Lori."

"Who'll deal with Walter?" she snapped.

"It looks to me like Walter is getting out of control. I believe he'll self-destruct."

"Maybe, but how much damage will he do in the mean time?"

Good question.

"Do you know a guy by the name of Edward Nordstrom?"

"No, should I?"

"He says he works for Walter. He may be one of his 'goon.'"

"The only members of Walter's goon squad I know are the ones that hung out with Walter and travelled with Mr. Simpson. They were always hanging around the office. I've never met anyone named Nordstrom."

"This guy is coming here to meet with me tomorrow evening. It should prove interesting. If he lied about his name, you may know him. Can you stay late?"

"OK, but I have my yoga class at seven o'clock."

"No problem. I just want you to greet him when he comes in. I'll be interested to see if you know him. Then you can go."

"Speaking of interesting, I've been trying to read my bible."

I grinned. "That is interesting. How's it going?"

"I haven't got a clue."

"Do you have a red letter edition?" I asked her.

"I don't even know what that is."

"It's a type of bible with all the words spoken by Jesus, printed in red letters."

"Yeah, I think mine's that way."

"You might want to read what Jesus had to say, or you might want to read your way through a whole book, like the book of Romans or one of the Gospels."

"What are the Gospels?" She asked.

"The first four books of the New Testament are

Matthew, Mark, Luke, and John. Each of them is a first-hand account of their individual experiences with Jesus. The word 'gospel' actually means 'good news.' So the gospels are the 'good news' about the life of Christ, as told by each of those men, who were personally acquainted with Jesus."

"I thought the word 'gospel' meant 'truth,' like when someone says something is "the gospel truth.""

"The word gospel has come to be thought of that way, because the four gospels, the 'good news,' are true accounts of the life of Christ."

"Huh, you learn something new, every day." She mused.

I grinned. "God willing."

"So, you think I should read one of the Gospels, which one?"

"Whichever one you want, all of them, eventually. You'll find they all tell the same basic story, with some unique observations from the different perspectives of the individual men."

"Are you saying these guys, Matthew, Mark, Luke, and John, were all real people, who actually lived during the time when Jesus was walking around teaching?"

"Yep, they were men who actually knew Jesus. Jesus is a real person. There is no question about it. You can check it out in any legitimate history of the time."

Christine looked perplexed

"I guess I sort of knew that, once. I wonder why I forgot."

"It wasn't important to you before. It is now. Why do you suppose it's become important?"

She shrugged.

"I don't know for sure, maybe because it's so important to you."

"… Maybe." I said

CHAPTER 31

I had asked Tony to be there for the meeting with Mr. Nordstrom. I was hoping Nordstrom might tell us something about Walter's activities that would have criminal implications. All we needed was some information that linked Walter to a crime.

The three of us were sitting in my office the next afternoon, waiting for Edward Nordstrom to appear. The conversation had shifted to Lori's relationship with Walter. Christine was bringing us up to speed on the latest developments.

"… They've met Walter and they find him equally as charming as Lori does. I had a hard time convincing them that he's a snake in the grass."

"Wait a minute; did you say they've met Walter?" I asked.

"I know, right? I was shocked myself. Apparently Lori's parents were having dinner at Willow Brook country club, one evening, when Walter approached their table and introduced himself for the first time. He told them he had met Lori in our office and he was familiar with her remarkable 'story.' He indicated he wanted to support her 'recovery,' and told them he was 'counselling' her by telephone." Christine informed us.

"We never told him anything about Lori. She

must have told him herself." I said.

"I guess she must have. I'm really surprised. She's so ashamed of that part of her life, I would have expected her to keep it a secret, to the degree she can. She would barely talk to me about it. I can't understand why she would have told Walter anything."

At that point, Tony interrupted.

"So, let me see if I understand all this," Tony began. "Walter Farley works for Ted Simpson, the Simpson Oil and Gas Company's Ted Simpson. Mr. Farley is also the CEO of the World Wide Security Agency, which provides security for Simpson Oil and Gas, among others. Over the last several months, Walter Farley has bugged your office, put a transponder on your truck, and sent men to follow you everywhere you go. He met Lori in your office, and he's been wheedling his way into her life. Is that where we are, so far?"

"Pretty much," I replied.

"J.W., has it occurred to you, Walter Farley may have sent the hit man to kill you last spring?"

I nodded. "I expect he probably did."

"What? Somebody tried to kill you, when did this happen?" Christine asked

"It was back in the spring, about the time you quit working for Simpson Oil and Gas."

"My god, what happened?"

"A guy followed me into an ally and tried to shoot me."

"How... I mean, what... did you do?" she asked.

"I shot him."

"Did you..."

"Yes, Christine. He missed, I didn't. He died of a gunshot wound, I didn't. It was a very near thing."

She was as white as a sheet.

"I'm sorry you had to hear that, Christine."

She blinked away some tears. Then she began to harden her countenance.

"That little weasel sent someone to kill you, because you took me on a date?"

"No, Christine, this isn't about you. You're part of it, I'm part of it, and now Lori is part of it, but this is all about Walter. He has to be the biggest and the best. He can't lose, and he can't be made to face the truth. He is a sociopath. He lies, manipulates, exaggerates, cheats, and plays dirty to get what he wants. He'll cut down anyone who gets in his way. He doesn't care about anyone but himself."

"We've got to put a stop to this," Tony said.

"We don't have any concrete evidence against him. Maybe, when Mr. Nordstrom gets here, he'll be able to give us something useful. He's running late." I pointed out. "Christine, how did you convince the Murphys they needed to keep Lori away from Walter?"

She was lost in thought, not really listening.

"Huh? Oh, that's just it. I'm not sure they were, convinced I mean. I let them know Walter has a history with us. I told them he's trying to do us harm, by trying to use Lori against us in some way. They said, as they've gotten to know him a little, they've come to trust him. To them, he seems very sincere and charming."

"It bothers me the Murphys seem to trust Farley, more than they trust y'all." Tony said.

It bothered me too.

"Maybe I could say something to her folks, J.W." Tony offered.

"Actually, Tony, that's a really good idea. Thanks."

"Even if her parents can be convinced Lori should stay away from him. She's both naïve and stubborn. She thinks she's all grown up and able to make her own decisions. She might not listen to her parents." Christine pointed out.

"She also thinks you have something against Walter, personally, Christine." I said.

"Well, that's fair enough. I do, now more than ever."

"But, from her teenage girl perspective, she might think you're just being vindictive. Walter can probably play her like a violin. She is the perfect puppet for his games."

We all considered the implications of the situation, for a moment.

"So, tell me more about this Nordstrom guy." Tony said.

"He's twenty six years old. He's been working for WWSA for two years, since he got out of the Marine Corp. Until about three months ago, WWSA had him working in Africa as part of a unit providing security for a relief agency. When that contract closed, he was recalled to Tyler, presumably to work on the Simpson detail. He told me Walter hasn't been able to pay his people on time. Nordstrom says he wants to come to work for me. It strikes me as odd. There are several big security outfits with Federal contracts who would probably hire Nordstrom, in a heart-beat. I'm sure I could get him on with Stryker/Knight Strategic or Sun Eagle Security Systems. If he turns out to be legit, that's what I'll do for him.

"He's late. You did say six o'clock, didn't you?" Christine asked.

I looked at my watch, it was nearly six thirty.

"Yeah, he is late. Say, Christine, you'd better run along if you're going to make your yoga class."

"Right, well I think I'd rather be here for this interview, if it's all right with y'all."

Tony nodded. "Fine with me," he said.

Uh huh, I saw the way Tony looked at Christine. That was interesting, very interesting. Christine had planned to go on to her yoga class, until Tony showed up for the meeting.

"Sure, Christine, glad to have you here. I warned him to be prepared for some tough questions. Nobody can ask tough questions, like a committee," I said.

Mr. Edward Nordstrom didn't answer any of our questions.

He never showed up.

CHAPTER 32

The press was in hog heaven with the Whitaker Trial. We had network and cable television coverage and all the media attention was the talk of the town. Tony and I were temporary pop idols again, the hero cop and his private detective sidekick. We were besieged by reporters and those parasites who love celebrity. I had not missed the attentions of the media over the last few months. I really hated getting it now.

Christine was overwhelmed with phone calls, most of them from media types or people who just wanted to speak to someone famous. We hired an answering service.

Tony called on my private line and asked me to come see him in his office. He said it was official business, and we could both avoid the media if I came downtown, to the Tyler Police Headquarters. When I walked in to Tony's partitioned office, he was reading the newspaper. I could see the front page.

"I swear, if I see my picture in the paper, one more time, I'll go see a plastic surgeon," I said.

"Lot of good that'll do you, J.W., you'll end up

looking like a comic cartoon of yourself."

"I've never seen a photo in which I didn't look pasty and fat. The media makes no attempt at being flattering." I said.

"Get over yourself. Of course, if you looked like me, you'd have no cause to whine."

He grinned.

"Tony, if I looked like you, I'd wear a bag over my head." I observed.

"J.W., sit down. I've got some bad news for you this morning. Did you see the story about the un-identified DB found in an alley by the waste man-agement people, early this morning?"

"Male, Caucasian, mid-twenties, single gunshot wound to the head? Yeah, I did. Let me guess, you have identification."

He nodded, silently.

"Is it Edward Nordstrom?"

"… Yep."

"I was afraid of that."

Tony nodded again "Now we have a full blown homicide investigation. This should help bring some things into focus, pretty quickly. We have de-tectives interviewing all of his known associates, including his boss, one Walter Farley, and his boss, Ted Simpson."

"Walter brought it on himself."

"Whoa there, pardner, we don't have anything on him, yet."

"Not yet, but the guy will make a mistake. He's a loose cannon. Now, it's just a matter of time."

"J.W., you need to watch your back. Nordstrom's body was found in the same alley where you shot that guy Hudson. He wasn't shot there, he was dumped there. Does that send a message?"

I nodded my silent response.

"I have a connection with you, J.W., and you're going to be treated as a suspect because of your connection to the previous shooting in the same alley. I have to bow out of this investigation. You caught a break though; the preliminary on the body suggests Nordstrom was probably killed late yesterday afternoon, or early in the evening. You didn't hear that from me, J.W. Oddly enough, as it works out, Christine and I are your alibis for that time. I believe Christine was with you all afternoon, and the three of us had dinner together, after Nordstrom didn't show up for his appointment. I can't say anymore. I have to direct you to the detective in charge of this investigation."

"OK, I understand. Thanks, Tony, I never intended to complicate your life with this mess. I see what you're doing for me here, and I appreciate it."

"No sweat. The department respects you. They won't get onto me for treating you with some courtesy, especially while all this media attention is going on. Are you ready to give a statement? Go to the third desk on the right, on your way out. Ask for Detective Reynolds."

Detective Reynolds was about thirty five. He was at least six feet tall and appeared to be a recovering steroid user. He had the kind of heavy muscling that comes from spending all your free time lifting weights. He also had a pronounced brow and visible acne. His head was shaved, a popular look for cops these days. He had drifted away from the norm though. He sported a dark handlebar moustache, waxed and twisted, with a little soul patch under his lower lip. He had taken off his Jacket and he had his shirt collar unbuttoned with his sleeves rolled up. He wore no tie. The whole effect reminded me of the strong man in the circus. Of course the circus strong man didn't carry an H&K .40 caliber semi-auto, in a shoulder holster.

"... So, you're saying you never actually met Nordstrom, but you did speak with him on the phone. On what days and at what times did you speak to him?"

"I spoke with him only one time, the day before yesterday. He called me. We set an appointment time for 6 PM, yesterday evening. We were supposed to meet in my office. He didn't show up for the appointment."

"Did he say why he wanted to meet with you?"

"He indicated he wanted a job."

"Are you hiring?"

"I'm often in need of people, usually part time, but these days I have more work piling up than there are people to do it."

"Where were you, from say, 4:00 pm until about 8:00 pm, yesterday?"

"I was in my office from about 2:30, until about 7:00 pm. Then I went out to dinner with friends."

"Did anyone see you at your office?

"My Office Administrator, Christine Valakova, was constantly there. I had appointments there with an insurance company representative at 3 PM, another appointment at 4 pm with the client of an attorney for whom I do some work. Like I said, I was at the office from about 2:30 until about 7:00 pm."

"I'll need the names and contact numbers for those people."

"OK, I'll be happy to provide them."

"You said you went out to dinner with friends. Who did you have dinner with?"

"…With Christine and Tony Escalante. Oh yeah, I forgot to mention that Tony came to the office at about 5:45."

"Detective Lieutenant Escalante?" He asked.

"That's right. He and Christine were both with me from about 5:45 until about 8:30 last night. Of course there were a lot of people at the restaurant who saw us together. We seem to attract a lot of attention these days. Oh, I also have the credit card receipt."

"OK, no further questions at this time. I expect you'll be available if we need to ask additional questions?"

"Yes, I will, Detective Reynolds. I'm not going anywhere."

As I was driving back to the office I reflected on how Walter Farley had come into our lives. I started wondering about how he had come into the life of Ted Simpson.

A few hours later, as my research began to pay off, I figured I knew.

It seems when Walter had been working for the competing oil company up in Oklahoma, he had engaged in a little corporate espionage. At that time, doing horizontal drilling and hydraulic fracturing of hard shale was a new use of an old technology. Whoever had the latest scientifically proven technology had a distinct advantage over the competition. Walter was fired for "mishandling" sensitive technical data. He must have shopped that data to Simpson. No wonder Simpson Oil and Gas Company got a technological jump on the industry!

Now the question was how Walter had approached Simpson, and why Simpson trusted Walter.

… After all, "Once a thief…"

Yet, Ted Simpson had told me he valued Walter for his loyalty. Why would Ted Simpson expect Walter to be loyal to him, when he had proven to be treacherous to others? Had Simpson really provided the start-up capital for WWSA? Why would he do that? Had he funded WWSA as a payoff for the stolen technical data? Had he bought Walter's loyalty? Could Walter be loyal to anyone other than himself?

My phone rang. It was Tony.

"I just got a call from a friend in the Sheriff's Department, J.W. You're not going to believe this. After sitting in the County jail for the last several weeks waiting for his trial date, somebody just now bailed our friend Orlando Cruz, out of jail!"

"Really, who made his bail?"

"It was a local attorney. Apparently he's been retained to represent the little peckerwood." Tony indicated.

"That's odd. I didn't think he had anybody who would be interested in helping him."

"I didn't either, J.W. And, it's no small amount of money. His bail was set at two hundred and fifty thousand dollars. Somebody had to come up with twenty five thousand dollars in cash, to bond him out. It's even stranger, because he's been sitting in jail for weeks. His trial is only a couple weeks away. If somebody was going to bail him out, why did they wait all this time to do it?" Tony wondered.

I thought about it.

"Thanks Tony. The bad news is he's on the loose, here in Tyler. The good news is we know about it in time to warn the Murphys."

CHAPTER 33

In discussing the situation with the Murphy family, we decided that for Lori's safety, she would move back into Christine's apartment. She had her own car and she could commute to her new school, without Orlando ever knowing where she was.

"She'll be quite safe at school; the private campus is hidden away back in the woods, behind security gates. To err on the side of caution, we'll alert the staff and they'll take extra security measures for her protection. They'll make sure she has an escort to and from the parking lot. The school has very good security; no one comes on or off the campus without being observed. Visitors need passes, so there is little chance he could get to her, even if he knew she was there."

"I can't believe we're going through all this again. You promised us Orlando wouldn't ever be a problem again. Walter may be right; you people are starting to look like amateurs. Walter could probably do a better job of protecting her. He owns a professional security company; he and his staff are experts at protecting people. He even has armored cars to transport people. If Lori wasn't insisting she'll be safe with you, we'd send her with him." Mrs. Murphy said.

I took a deep breath.

Was this his game? We had beaten him to the punch, just barely. If Walter had contacted the Murphys with the news about Orlando, before we did…

God is good.

"Mr. Murphy, I think taking advantage of Walter's security service is a great idea. You don't want to be worrying about Orlando showing up at your house again. You tell Walter you want him to provide constant protection for you and your wife, while we protect Lori."

Christine looked at me like she thought I was crazy.

My idea was to protect Lori's parents. I figured Walter would have to make absolutely certain they stayed safe, in order to make himself look and feel powerful, competent, successful and important.

It's always nice to kill two birds with one stone.

"That's exactly what we're going to do. I'm glad to see you extending some professional respect and courtesy. We'll call Walter right away."

As we were leaving the Murphy house, I rode with Lori in her car, she was driving. Christine was following behind us in her car.

"Lori, I know you and Walter have become friends. I have to ask, why did you want to come with us, instead of going with Walter?"

She thought about it for a moment.

"I don't know exactly. It just felt like it was the right thing to do…"

"His sheep know His voice." I thought.

"… Besides, it was you who got me back from Orlando in the first place. Somehow, I can't see Walter being able to handle something like that. I mean he talks big, and he boasts about things, but… I don't know. Somehow you seem more solid. You don't brag, you just get stuff done. I feel like I can trust you."

"Yes, you can."

She looked over at me and smiled. "I know."

I smiled back.

"It was you who told me I could make it. You're the one who convinced me God still loved me, even after..." She trailed off.

I nodded. "I haven't ever lied to you."

"No, you were right. Even when I didn't believe you, or when I didn't like what you said, you've never lied to me."

"Has Walter lied to you?"

"I don't know, maybe. He's said some things that were... that seemed... wrong, somehow. Especially the things he said about you, and he was confusing when he talked about God."

I was surprised.

"I wouldn't have imagined Walter had much to say about God."

"Walter said, God is in everything and everything is God. Because of that, there is no right or wrong. No good or evil, because everything is good. If it seems right to us, then it is right for us. I don't know... Does that make sense?"

"Well, yes and no. It's partly true and mostly wrong. It is true God is in everything, it is not true everything is God. Let me give you an example. A great artist puts something of themselves into their work. They even sign their name to the work. When you see their work you see some part of them, there is a little bit of the artist in all of their work. But, you wouldn't look at the art work and say the art is the artist, would you?"

"No, of course not."

"God is the Creator of all things, but the things He created are not Him. By looking at His creation, we learn some things about God, but we are not actually seeing God."

"Yeah, I get that."

"So then right and wrong, good and evil, are not based on our personal opinions. They are part of the work of God. He has determined what is right and good, He has also determined what is wrong or evil. If you want to know what God has determined about those things, it's all there in the Bible."

We drove along in silence for a few minutes, each thinking our own thoughts.

Suddenly, Lori had something to say.

"I'm really looking forward to seeing "Tummy Tum-Tum!" She beamed.

When we got to Christine's apartment, I caught her eye and she smiled with a little shake of her head. It told me we hadn't been followed.

"Mr. Tumescence," Christine's cat, met us at the door. "Tummy" rubbed all over Lori's leg and flopped down on his side to be petted. Lori's room was exactly as she had left it. It had become her home, away from home.

"Ladies, it's late in the day. I'm going to go by the office and check my messages. Tomorrow is Saturday, what will y'all do over the weekend?"

"Well, the pool is still open. This is the last weekend. We'll probably take advantage of the pleasant weather and hang out at the pool, or in the clubhouse. How does that sound, Lori?"

"Super, I have some homework and a report that's due on Monday, so I'll work on it and catch a tan, out by the pool."

"Alright, unless our plans change, Lori, next week, Christine will take you to school. After school, one of us will meet you in the parking lot, and you'll come straight to the office for the rest of the day. You can do your homework there."

"OK, Boss man, whatever you say."

"I don't know at this point, how long we'll have to keep up this routine. I'll find out for sure when Orlando is scheduled to stand trial. We'll work it out."

At the office, I found most of the phone messages to be requests for interviews or obvious ploys to get attention, especially the last one.

"Well played, Mr. Tucker. I'll be in touch."

I recognized the voice.

It was Walter's.

CHAPTER 34

I spent the weekend at my hunting lease, making minor repairs to my little trailer and my hunting blinds, cleaning out wasp nests and spiders, and fishing in the pond. I love the smell of the deep woods in the fall. I had some great pictures on my game cameras. There were hogs, coyotes, bobcats, raccoons and several deer frequenting the feeder areas and the pond. One pretty nice buck was seen in both locations. I was looking forward to wearing my camouflage into the woods, and watching the world wake up on some chilly morning in the not too distant future. During the season I would spend every weekend here, hunting ducks and deer.

Monday put me right back in the rat race.

I learned Ted Simpson had almost certainly provided the start-up capital for Walter's new business venture. The timing suggested it had been payment for the stolen technical drilling data.

Walter had started the World Wide Security Agency, investing a huge sum of money in start-up capital. Initially it was a modest undertaking, fully funded. Then he had started spending and borrowing a vast amount of cash. He used the money to entertain various government insiders, to help land his contracts and to recruit and equip a small army of security agents. He purchased custom armored personnel carriers designed to withstand improvised explosive devices or IEDs as they are now commonly known. His first couple of contracts proved highly profitable, but he squandered the money on a corporate headquarters office in New York, for his Strategic International Corporation, expensive high profile advertising, traveling around the world to promote his company, bribes, and dirty tricks against his competition.

After talking with a number of creditors, bureaucrats, politicians, and former employees, I learned several things. Walter spent money much faster than he made it. He failed to properly service his debt, but worse was his inability to keep his elaborate promises and lies.

Powerful people began to realize Walter was lying to them. Soon, he was no longer able to get really lucrative contracts. He still had the same level of debt and overhead, but the revenues were decreasing. Walter had to close his fancy office in New York City. He had to let some of his people go. His last security contract had just been terminated. Most of his security people had quit. He had to sell off equipment he had paid top dollar for.

Today, his only real client seemed to be Simpson Oil and Gas Company. It appeared he had to take the Personal Assistant job with Ted Simpson, because he could no longer afford to pay himself his own salary. Strategic International Corporation was dead, and the WWSA was barely a shell of its former self.

Why would Ted Simpson continue to support him

at all? If everyone he had ever done business with, including Christine and I, could see Walter for what he really was, why couldn't Simpson? What hold did Walter have on Mr. Simpson? Was it some form of extortion? There must be something other than Ted Simpson's belief that Walter was "intensely loyal."

Mr. Simpson had offered me the job as head of security for Simpson Oil and Gas Company. Why? What did that mean?

It meant it was time for me to talk with Ted Simpson about these things.

He agreed to meet with me, later the same evening at his home in south Tyler. He had to give me precise directions, because the house was hidden and gated against uninvited guests. His home was only three or four miles from my office, on a busy feeder road I drove on frequently. I marveled that I had driven past the little driveway which disappeared into the forest, probably hundreds of times, and never knew it was the entrance to a magnificent estate. All of the neighbors surrounding them lived in huge houses in swanky, up-scale subdivisions, with grand, gated stone entranceways, with names like RAVENCREST or STONECLIFFE. The simple driveway entrance to the Simpson place was virtually invisible between those ostentatious outcroppings.

Mr. Simpson had his own security gates a few hundred feet up his driveway. I pushed the button on the intercom at the gates, and they swung open without anyone speaking to me. I saw the cameras, so I knew someone could see me. It was interesting that none of Walter's security people were to be seen at the gates.

Ted Simpson and his wife of more than thirty years, Corinne, lived in a modest French château of about sixteen thousand square feet. It was three stories of granite and wrought iron under a verdigris copper roof with multiple chimneys. I wondered if they were looking forward to multiple fires, in multiple fireplaces. The Château Simpson sat at the edge of a three or four acre pond, with a fountain shooting a geyser, thirty feet into the air. The house was situated on about twenty acres of manicured landscaping, with a tennis court out back, just beyond the swimming pool. My view of those amenities was partly blocked by the six car garage, attached to the house by a Porte cache. Somehow, this magnificent minor castle was the only single family home in the area. All of their neighbors in those exclusive subdivisions had big homes too, of course, but they were mostly crowded together within the confines of their tiny one and two acre lots.

I parked in the circular driveway, rather than under the Porte cache, and walked up the wide sidewalk to the massive front doors. I figured the side door under the Porte cache was just for the family and the help.

As I pushed the doorbell, and listened to the chimes, I imagined there were probably very few times anyone ever rang the bell.

The door was opened by a servant whom I suspected might be called the butler.

The foyer I observed inside the front door had polished marble floors and was so huge that in another time it might have been called a ballroom. Sure, it had polished marble floors, but I doubted anyone ever danced there. I gave the butler my card.

"How do you do, Mr. Tucker, Mr. Simpson is expecting you. He's in the library, please follow me."

I was glad he hadn't said "walk this way," because he walked kind of slow and funny.

The library was in fact, a library. I estimated the number of books to be at least a thousand titles, most of them bound in leather and some of them rare or first edition. It was an oak panelled room, two stories tall, with books in shelves on three walls, both downstairs and upstairs. The fourth wall was mostly occupied by a massive stone fireplace. There were polished wrought iron and brass ladders at each end of the room, by which, I assumed one could gain access to the second floor of the library. It was part of the second floor of the house, but in the library, it was more of a balcony, about six feet wide running all the way around the three walls above. It appeared the floor of the balcony had been designed and engineered in such a way, the book shelves below provided the support for the floor above. I could see a door between bookshelves in one wall up there, which probably led out into the rest of the second floor.

Even though we were enjoying the balmy warm days of fall folks tend to call "Indian summer", there was a gas fire going in the fireplace.,

I found Mr. Simpson seated in a massive, over-stuffed, brown leather armchair, next to the fireplace. He didn't stand, but rather pointed at the matching arm chair opposite his.

"Sit down, boy. Can I buy you a drink? I'm drinking single malt."

I sat down as instructed.

"No thank you, sir. It's a little early in the day for me."

"Fine, what brings you to my neck of the woods?"

"Mr. Simpson, I need to ask you some questions about Walter."

He nodded, and looked over at the butler.

"Henry, will you please ask Mrs. Simpson to join us."

After Henry left, I started to say something, but Mr. Simpson held up his hand.

"Hold on, boy, I think we'll wait for Corinne, before we start this discussion."

"Mr. Simpson, I'm not sure your wife needs to hear what we'll be discussing."

"I'm pretty sure I don't care what you think she needs to hear." He mumbled.

We stared at each other for a moment.

"Why would you want your wife to be a part of this discussion?"

"Does it have anything to do with my political plans?"

"I don't know, probably. I need to talk to you about Walter."

"Well then, she needs to be here."

"Why?"

"… Because, Walter Farley is our son," Corinne Simpson said, from the doorway.

CHAPTER 35

As she came into the room, I stood up to greet Corinne Simpson.

"How do you do, Mr. Tucker, Walter has told me quite a lot about you."

She was tall and slim, wearing black pants and a white blouse with long sleeves. Her hair was still blonde, though I suspected she used some form of chemical enhancement. I could tell there had been other enhancements as well. She was no stranger to cosmetic surgery. She had a Barbie doll body that didn't match her age, and her face had the stiff, sort of polished look which comes from too much time under the knife. Her eyebrows were tattooed. Either as a result of the surgeries or the application of Botox, she was unable to show any facial expression. The whole effect was like talking to someone who was wearing a mask.

But then, we all wear masks, don't we?

"I'm pleased to meet you, Ma'am."

She extended her hand and when I took it, it was as cold as ice.

"Mr. Simpson, I believe I'll take that drink now." I said.

He chuckled and pointed to an assortment of bottles on a shelf next to the fireplace. There was glassware stacked behind them.

"There's an ice maker in the cabinet down there, help yourself."

"Can I get you anything, Mrs. Simpson?" I offered.

I figured Henry, the butler, wasn't going to be joining us.

"I guess about two fingers of Bourbon won't kill me." She replied

"... On the rocks?"

"No, neat is fine."

Soon, we were seated and settled down to discuss the matter at hand.

"Corinne, this fella is like a badger, once he takes a hold of something, he just won't let go of it."

"So I'm told," she smiled, coldly.

"Mr. Simpson I have a lot of questions..." I started.

"Yep, I expect you do. First, let me ask you one." Ted Simpson interrupted.

I nodded and simply said, "OK.".

"Why the hell didn't you just go away and leave us alone. I figured writing you a check and telling you 'good bye' would settle the matter."

I considered how to respond.

"I intended to, but Walter wouldn't leave me alone."

They looked at each other, and Mr. Simpson sighed.

"Now it's my turn. Why did you hire me to run a background check on you?" I asked.

"I told you, I'm about to make a run at the Governorship. Corinne suggested it would be a good idea to see what kind of a mess our opposition might be able to stir up."

"OK, but why me, there are plenty of other agencies with better resources?"

"Walter recommended you. He wanted to do it himself, but he realized he already knew everything that might be pertinent. We needed a disinterested third party. So he suggested you."

I still wondered why he had picked me, instead of a bigger firm.

"Did he say why?"

"Not really, just that he had heard you were thorough. He was right, you are thorough." He observed.

"Why does Walter have the last name Farley? Does it have something to do with your absence from college for part of a semester?"

Mr. Simpson got red in the face.

"Damn, boy, you seem to know all the answers. Why ask the question?"

I looked at Mrs. Simpson.

"Ted left school, because he needed to deal with aspects of a little indiscretion in his youthful life. He had fathered a child with an underage girl. Ted was in love with her and wanted to marry her, but his father wouldn't permit it. Ted actually left school to sneak off to be with her, when the baby was born. She had the baby and then her parents threatened to expose the situation to the media and the authorities. Ted's father handled the matter by bribing the young woman's family to keep quiet. Ted returned to college the next semester. He continued to support Ms. Farley and their son, often visiting them, even after he and I were married."

I nodded. "Yeah, when I finally talked to your college roommate, he told me part of the story. I didn't know the girl's name, and I didn't know Walter was that baby."

I thought of another question.

"Mr Simpson, why didn't you marry the girl, when she came of age?"

"I was already married, to Corinne."

I thought about what I had just learned. How

young had the Farley girl been?

"Ted's father felt I would be a more suitable choice for Ted," Mrs. Simpson added.

"Yeah, and I learned real quick, he was right about that," Ted Simpson said, winking at Corinne.

"Mrs. Simpson, you said Walter is 'our' son. How did you come to think of him as your son?"

"We... that is to say I, am unable to have children. Walter's mother was killed in an automobile accident when Walter was eleven. He came to live with us. He's the closest thing to a son I will ever have."

"Yes, ma'am, I understand. Are you aware that Walter has some mental health issues?"

She smiled sadly. "Mr. Tucker, Walter is a sociopath. He is the most damaged and dangerous person I have ever known."

Mr. Simpson reached over and took his wife's hand.

"Well, there you have it, boy. You got to the bottom of the story." He said.

"Mr. Simpson, Walter is your biggest liability. It appears he stole the technical specs for your horizontal drilling and fracturing from a competing company. You funded a business for him and he ran it into the ground. He's trying to get back on top, and he sees me as his competition. Over the last several months, he's bugged my office, planted a transponder on my truck, sent men to follow me, and generally interfered with me, on several levels."

"Well, I'm real sorry about your luck. He's just like you in that way, he won't let go once he gets a bite."

"Let me be clear. If you run for political office, it will all come out. Walter is headed for self-destruction, and he may very well pull you down with him."

He nodded. "Yeah, I see that. I was hopeful all this would blow over. It's not his fault, you know?

He can't help it. He's real smart, did great in school. Smarts ain't the problem. He's got a screw loose. I was hoping some time spent in the military would help him learn some self-discipline, but it didn't help. He came out even more twisted."

Simpson stopped to take a deep pull on his Scotch. Then he started talking again.

"Walter got the job up in Oklahoma, because I recommended him. I didn't know he was going to steal proprietary information. I've tried to help him and get help for him, but he can't be controlled. I set him up with his own business, because I knew he could never run Simpson Oil and Gas. I'll see he's taken care of, but he'll never control any part of the company. The stockholders must come first."

I noticed his last word had sounded like "firsh-ht," because the single malt was kicking in.

We sat in silence for a moment.

"Why did you offer me the job as your head of security? Walter has his people providing security for you."

He shook his head. "Walter's boys, the ones he has left, are basically just body guards. I don't really need them. I need cyber security and overall corporate security, to manage all aspects of our corporate risk. I figured you were better qualified."

"What made you think Walter would have tolerated that?"

"Hell, boy, do you think I give a flying fig about Walter's personal pride. I run one of the largest and most successful independent oil and gas E&P companies in the United States. We have a board of directors, with me as the Chairman of the Board and CEO, to make decisions about the future of our company. I didn't know Walter was going to fixate on you as his personal enemy, but since he did, you can consider the offer withdrawn."

I could tell he was more than a little bit drunk.

"Well, where do we go from here?" I asked.

"We're going to bed. You can go on home, or go to hell, for all I care," he slurred.

I nodded and stood up.

"There's one other thing I think you should be aware of. You know about the investigation into the murder of Edward Nordstrom, the man who worked for Walter. I'm quite sure Walter killed him, or he had it done. And, I'm pretty sure he sent a man to kill me, earlier this year. I tell you this to let you know how desperate he is. This is not going to end well for him."

"Get the hell out of my house," Mr. Simpson spat. "And, I'd watch my back if I were you."

"You'll have to excuse my husband's manners, Mr. Tucker. He's just upset his political ambitions may not be realized," Mrs. Simpson said, as she stood up to show me to the door. "He's rather used to getting what he wants."

"Yes," I said, looking down at Mr. Simpson, where he sat slumped in the big arm chair. "And 'the apple don't fall far from the tree'."

CHAPTER 36

Trudy Gerhardt was missing. At least she was missing from her home. Technically I had been hired by Bobby Gerhardt, her nine-year-old son. He wanted to know where his mommy went.

It was the usual thing; Mrs. Gerhardt packed up some of her stuff one day and drove away. Bobby was left with his dad, and a lot of questions. Tom Gerhardt was too confused and heartsick to explain anything to Bobby. He didn't know where his wife had gone either.

Tom was the man paying the bill, but little Bobby was our client.

Christine's diligent research eventually found Trudy Gerhardt, down near Houston. She was living with a guy named Brad Townsend, a man she had "met" on the internet.

Four hours of driving in the rain, brought me to a lovely residence in a huge, planned living development called "The Woodlands." I rang the doorbell.

The lady who answered the door was a reasonably attractive brunette, whom I recognized immediately from the pictures Bobby and his dad had shown me.

"Hello, Mrs. Gerhardt. My name is John Wesley Tucker, Bobby sent me. I'd like to talk to you for a moment. May I come in?"

"Who… what… what do you mean, Bobby sent you?"

"Yes Ma'am, you remember Bobby, your son? Bobby called me and asked me to find you. Could we talk inside?"

Maybe it was because of the pouring rain, or maybe she wanted to know about Bobby, for whatever reason, she invited me in. I took off my raincoat. She made coffee while I wandered around in the den. When she returned with the coffee service, we sat and talked.

"How is Bobby?" She asked.

"He's confused, frightened and hurt, Mrs. Gerhardt. He wants to know you're alright. He wants to know if you're coming home. He wants to know why you left. He thinks he must have done something to make you so mad, you left without even saying goodbye."

She shook her head. "Kids get the strangest ideas."

"Why did you leave?"

She took a moment to consider her response. She took a deep breath and let it out slowly. Then she answered my question.

"I just got tired and bored. Tired of being a wife and mother, bored with the life I was living."

She went on to tell me about how she had "met" her internet lover. It had all started innocently enough; Brad Townsend was a friend of a friend on Facebook. Pretty soon they were chatting directly online, and progressed to phone conversations. It slowly evolved into adultery and a failed marriage.

It could be argued the marriage had already failed, and was the reason she had become attracted to the stranger on the internet.

"Did your husband mistreat you?" I asked her.

"Tom? Goodness no. He hasn't got the backbone for it. He has all the fire of a bowl of bread pudding. He just wasn't available. We never talked, and it had gotten to where we shared a bed, but only because we didn't have three bedrooms. It wasn't a marriage; it was more like we just tolerated each other."

"Will you be going home to Tom and Bobby?"

She shook her head again. "Not a chance. I'm finally starting to have some fun. Brad is a hoot. Why would I want to go back to boring old Tom?"

"What about Bobby?"

"We'll work something out. He can come visit me sometime." She suggested.

"Ma'am, are you a religious person?"

"What do you mean?" She asked.

"Do you go to church or synagogue?"

"Sure, sometimes, why do you ask?" She narrowed her eyes at me.

"Did you get married in a church?" I already knew the answer, because I had seen a wedding photo on the mantle in their home.

"Yes, we did, what's your point?"

"Just to remind you that you said vows in front of God and witnesses, promising you would never do what you're doing, right here, right now."

"That's none of your business." She said, standing up.

"Mrs. Gerhardt, you're still a married woman. Sometimes keeping a commitment is... difficult and unrewarding on a personal level, but ultimately essential for everyone involved. Wouldn't it be better for everyone if you went home and worked on your marriage?"

"Don't call me, Mrs. Gerhardt. My name is Trudy. The marriage is over. I've filed for a divorce from

Tom. I think it's time for you to go." She snapped.

I put my raincoat back on and headed for home, four more hours of driving in the rain.

As I drove, I thought about my meeting with Mrs. Gerhardt. I had recorded the meeting with a video camera built into a pen, which I had clipped into my shirt pocket. I was hoping I would have good, clear images to show Bobby. I wanted him to see that his mother was safe and healthy. I figured I would let the video answer his questions.

It probably wouldn't help much.

Back in my office I downloaded the video and saved it on a thumb drive. I found the whole thing very sad. It was typical of the times in which we live. She had been seduced by her own selfishness. It takes two to marry, but it only takes one to end a marriage. Sure, they were both responsible, in fact in some ways Tom Gerhardt was the most responsible person, but the point was she had chosen to end it. She had abandoned her husband and her son, to pursue her own personal happiness and pleasure.

Christine and I talked about it.

"Yeah, it's sad, but men do it all the time. Men are usually more deceptive and sneaky about it, but society seems to accept it when men do it. We only get bent out of shape when a woman does it." Christine observed.

"I know, Christine, it's part of my point. Society doesn't have the authority to decide what's right and wrong. Sin is sin. Man or woman. Just because we live in a time and place where pretty much anything goes, doesn't change the reality of right and wrong." I started "Humans have always been selfish. Everything a person does is right in their own eyes. If the criteria by which we establish law is nothing more than, 'if it feels right to you, then it is right for you', then there is no real basis for law. If a society decides stealing is a crime in this century, decade, or year, but changes its mind in the next, where is the truth? People want what they want, and if they can't have it, or can't do it legally, then they do it illegally, or work to change the law, so they can have it their way."

"Well, that's the way democracy works. 'We the people' get to determine our moral codes and laws, through our elected representatives." Christine answered.

"If 'we the people' don't acknowledge there is a higher authority upon which to base our laws, then there is no authority except general consensus. We live in a society with the general consensus of 'if it feels good, just do it'." I posited.

"No, we don't. We add the stipulation… 'so long as it doesn't hurt anyone'. Otherwise, it would mean anyone could do whatever they wanted, to whoever they wanted to do it to. It really would be chaos."

"Exactly, and when there is no real basis for law, other than 'so long as it doesn't hurt anyone', it leaves the door open for discussion about the definition of 'hurt', and the definition of 'anyone'. For several centuries slavery was accepted as normal, because some people decided some other people weren't 'people' but property, so slavery didn't 'hurt' them. We don't want to forget Hitler and the Nazis decided it would be a good idea to eradicate Jews, gypsies, and anyone else they deemed 'unsuitable', and the German society agreed."

"Sure, but other societies disagreed, and we fought a world war over it." Christine reminded me.

"We fought a world war partly because of how Hitler treated people, but it was mostly to stop his attempt at world domination. Just a few years later, the world turned a blind eye to Stalin's slaughter of millions of his own people. My point is, no society, or any group of societies can be trusted to determine right and wrong, without a higher authority. Maybe next time, they'll decide all redheaded people should be excluded from voting, or blue eyed people should be blinded, or religious people should have no legal rights."

"That's ridiculous." She replied.

"No, it's predictable. Our society has already decided people who are still in the womb aren't people."

Christine wasn't having it. "Oh sure, the abortion issue, you religious types always come back to it, don't you?" She sneered.

"What I'm saying is, if societies have the power to make law based on nothing more than consensus, watch your back. Next week, they may be coming for you."

"Wow, you really are paranoid."

"No, Christine, I'm not. Look to the lessons of history. God established laws so we could see our inability to live in obedience, constantly choosing to indulge our selfish desires. We fail individually and as societies. History has proven that societies and cultures fail when they abandon traditional moral beliefs, and they all do, eventually."

"Well, isn't that because of the second law of thermodynamics, entropy, or something?" she asked.

I laughed.

"Chaos is more likely to naturally occur than order? Organized systems tend to become disorganized? Heat or energy tends to dissipate over time? A parked car doesn't improve by sitting idle in the weather for decades. Sure, those terms you mentioned are scientific principles to describe the process. Eventually, everything decays. The Bible calls it the law of sin and death. One thing leads to the other." I agreed. "It isn't the way it was supposed to go, but original sin started the process. The bible also says 'the Law of the Spirit of life, in Christ Jesus has set me free from the law of sin and death. There is therefore now no condemnation for those who are in Christ Jesus.' That means we can overcome selfish desire and come into obedience to God's law, not through our own righteousness, but through Christ's having paid the penalty for our disobedience. So long as we live like animals ignoring the law of God, and making our own laws based on what feels good, we have separated ourselves from His perfect order. We have embraced a life which leads to chaos. We will die in sin. When we surrender to God, we become born again as new spiritual persons, the old has passed away." I concluded.

"John, why is it, every time I have a discussion with you, you start talking about God?" Christine asked.

"I can't talk about law and order without addressing the basis for morality. I am a servant of God. Somebody once said, 'If there is no God then nothing really matters. If there is a God, then nothing else matters'. He is the Alpha and Omega, the beginning and the end."

"Well, it sure seems to crop up in any conversation we have, John. You're kind of a religious nut job."

"Oh, it's worse than you know. I'm an Ambassador of the Kingdom of heaven. This world is not my home."

She rolled her eyes. "See? Exactly what I'm saying, when you talk like that…"

I grinned at her.

While I'm aware such discussions can become uncomfortable for people, sometimes I have to clearly state my mission on earth.

CHAPTER 37

As I was driving to the shooting range, I spotted Dustin pushing his cart along, so I pulled over to talk to him.

"You gots to confront that devil face to face," Dustin said. "He don't like it, so you gots to do it."

Today he was still wearing his sweatshirt, as usual, but at least the weather was starting to get cooler.

"Is that what you do, Dustin?"

"Naw suh, it's not my fight."

"It's everyone's fight. Sooner or later, everyone has to choose which side they're on. Unless or until you choose to serve the Lord, you are already serving the devil."

"Oh, He knows that I knows who's I am, but I'm too wounded in the head to be in the battle," he said, tapping his head. "But you, Mr. Angel, you is in the battle. You can't get lazy, and you can't fall asleep."

"I get tired, Dustin. Sometimes I just want to take some time off and let the world go on, without my interference for a while"

He laughed.

"Ole devil don't need to kill you, or take you prisoner. He just needs you to quit fighting."

I nodded again. "Somebody once said 'all it takes

for evil to prevail is for good men to do nothing'."

Dustin narrowed his eyes at me.

"Most folks don't even know there is a battle. They just wants to be left alone, long as they got their TV to entertain um, feed um lies and make um stupid. They follow that devil like sheep, doin' what he want um to do." He said.

"Some people know what's going on." I pointed out.

"Maybe so, but they figure the politicians and preachers can fight the good fight, so they don't have to choose up sides, but you, Mr. Angel, you is in the battle."

"You can't win if you don't fight." I pointed out.

"I can't fight no more." He replied.

"Sure you can, Dustin, as long as you speak the truth, and as long as you watch and pray, you're in the fight."

"Oh, I is watching and praying, sho nuff."

I clapped him on the back.

"I know you are. You see a lot, and you always speak the truth."

"I got me my rounds, Good Angel. You watch your back. That devil means to ambush you," Dustin informed me as he set his cart in motion.

So, as usual I was still enjoying my conversations with a homeless crazy person. Oddly, his advice is usually far more sensible than any of the expert talking heads on the television and radio. But then, I know where the message comes from, on both sides.

Back in my car, I continued on to meet Tony and Christine at the shooting range.

"Hey, Christine, I want you try this out," I said, as I pulled the Taurus "Judge" revolver out of my bag.

"It's a popular home defense gun, because it shoots both .410 shotgun and .45 caliber shells. These low velocity shells make it safer for use indoors, especially in an apartment, where bullet penetration has to be contained."

She took it from me and hefted it.

"It's kind of heavy," she said.

"Yep, and even heavier when it's loaded. It's not a good concealed carry gun for most women, because of its size. However, it could be very useful in close quarters, if you were to keep it handy in your bedroom or wherever. Go ahead and load it. Put one or two .410 shells in, then .45s in the remaining chambers."

After she had it loaded, she fired on the target down range.

"Wow," she said, "I expected it to kick worse than that. The muzzle lift isn't too bad either."

Tony and I had been helping her with her shot placement. We were emphasizing muzzle control and improving her stance and breathing. She was getting better at longer ranges. With this gun though, longer ranges were not really a consideration. We saw that she had placed all five shots tight in the ten ring at fifteen feet.

"That'll do," Tony said. "Run a few more rounds through it. This time, try to reacquire your sight picture a little more quickly. The goal is to fire all of your shots just a bit faster, without losing accuracy."

Christine progressed quickly. She went from one shot per second, to five shots in about three seconds, all of them in the ten ring.

"Outstanding," Tony said. "I'd like to try it out."

He fired five rounds at twenty feet.

"I'm not a big fan of revolvers, but this is a fine weapon for its intended purpose." He said.

When we had all shot the gun, I gave it to Christine.

"I know you like revolvers. Keep it handy in your

bedroom, but don't tell anyone you have it. Do you use a housekeeper?" I asked her.

"Are you kidding me, John, on the salary you pay me? I'm the only housekeeper at my place. I've even given up on getting Lori to keep her room clean. She helps out in the kitchen occasionally, but that's about it."

I laughed.

"I told you having a teenage roommate would offer some challenges."

She rolled her eyes, "You have no idea!"

Tony interrupted.

"On that subject, J.W., Orlando's trial has been scheduled for Monday the twenty third of this month. That'll be the end of him; you'll only have to watch over Lori for a little more than a week."

"Oh, Tony, that's great news!" Christine said.

I nodded, grimly.

"What's the problem, John? You should be as thrilled as I am." Christine said.

"I guess so; I'll be glad to see Orlando put away, but it means things are speeding up."

"What things, J.W.?" Tony asked.

"I'm not exactly sure. How's the murder investigation coming along?"

"… Which one?" Tony asked.

"… The Edward Nordstrom murder." I reminded him.

"Not. We've got nothing, officially. We're pretty sure our person of interest, who we all know too well, had something to do with it, but we've got no hard evidence and he's unshakable under interrogation. It looks like this one may go on the books as an 'unsolved' cold case."

I shook my head. "No, Tony, he won't get away with it. He's been slippery and calculating, but he'll trip up. It's just a matter of time now. He's always been able to worm his way out of tight spots. He's deceived his teachers, employers, superiors, and anyone else he wanted to, all of his life, and he got away with it. He's very good when he's forced into a corner. I wonder if he would respond differently if he thought he was safe, and he was the one in control."

"We've tried that angle, J.W. We've used some very good interrogation techniques, even suggesting to him he was brilliant and superior to our investigative abilities, but he just acted smug. He never gives up anything useful. Believe me, he's a master at self-protection." Tony said.

"His whole life revolves around himself, and how clever and powerful he thinks he is. That's how he'll get himself nailed. He'll go too far and then he'll fall." I predicted.

"… From your mouth, to God's ear, J.W." Tony said.

I shrugged.
"We'll see."

CHAPTER 38

"How is your bible study coming along, Christine?"

We were at the office. Lori was at school.

"I'm kind of struggling." Christine replied.

"Struggling with what?"

"I'm struggling with Jesus."

I raised my eyebrows.

"What I mean is Jesus and God are talked about in the book of Luke as a matter of fact, suggesting Jesus and the Father are one, but I'm not sure I believe any of it." She said.

"Ahhh, there's the rub. Sooner or later everyone comes to that place. It comes down to belief. It comes down to faith. Have you read any of chapter ten, in Luke's gospel?"

She nodded silently in response.

"You might try praying and asking God to help you believe."

"How can I pray, if I don't believe?" She asked.

"God hears all prayers, whether you believe or not."

She thought about it for a moment.

"I guess I'm more practical than that." She suggested.

"Did Jesus claim to be the son of God?" I asked her.

"Yes." She stated, emphatically.

"Well then, practically speaking, there are only three possibilities. One, Jesus was crazy, completely irrational and just plain bonkers. I mean really, claiming to be the Son of God! Do you believe he was crazy?" I asked.

"No, I don't. He was far too organized and focused to be insane. If he were just crazy the religious leaders wouldn't have bothered with him. It would have become obvious and they would have just watched him as his followers quit and his movement fell apart. Instead, they hated him and plotted his death, to shut him up." She observed.

"Then, the next option is he was a liar, just pretending to be the Son of God to deceive people and get them to follow him. Do you believe he was lying?"

She shook her head, in response. "No, I don't."

"Well then, there is only one more option. He was telling the truth and he really is the son of God."

"I've heard that argument before, you know? What if all of it, the whole Bible is just a bunch of weird stories. I know it's unlikely, because the historic record supports so much of it. Are some parts true and other parts fable?

"Well, there's also the argument Jesus was just a political activist. There were a lot of them at the time. What do you think about that?" I asked her.

"If that were true, why would anyone bother to write so much about his life? Why would anyone care about a defeated political wanna-be, who died two thousand years ago in a seemingly insignificant place in the middle-east?" She asked.

"Perhaps he was just a great moral teacher." I suggested.

She considered the possibility for a moment.

"No, there have been any number of great moral teachers, but they are not maligned and hated the way Jesus was. The Jewish leaders wouldn't have convinced the Roman authorities to kill him, just for being a great moral teacher."

"We're getting kind of low on other options Christine. Why would the life of one man be the cause for so much change in the world? Why would people suffer and die over the course of more than two thousand years, for being followers of a man who died in a different time and place from them?"

That's exactly what I'm struggling with." She clarified.

I nodded. "It is the single most important decision you will ever make. There's a cost to be counted. A relationship with Christ is free for the asking, but it ain't cheap. Some people will think less of you. You will change. It will determine the course of your life, and your place in eternity."

"Yeah, I get that. There will be serious ramifications to whatever decision I make. What will our relationship be, you know... between you and me, if I say 'no'? She asked, tentatively.

"Christine, I didn't hire you with any hidden agenda or secret strings. Our relationship isn't based on what you choose to do with your knowledge of Christ. You are free to be you. I love you and appreciate you for all of your strengths and abilities, not to mention your extraordinary beauty. I'm here to help, but I don't have any requirements related to your personal decision."

She nodded. "OK, thanks."

"Just keep reading and believe in yourself. You're intelligent and discerning. You'll figure it out."

CHAPTER 39

I started to spend the weekend all alone in my little, old travel trailer on the hunting lease. Out there I had no phone service, no electricity and no worries. Being all alone was only the first part of my weekend plan that didn't work out.

I had a swarm of visitors.

Saturday morning, I woke up with fire ants in the trailer, and moving into my sleeping bag! There was a brief battle, involving close quarters and hand to hand combat, followed by me scrambling out of the sleeping bag, and ending with me spraying insect repellent all around the base of the trailer on the inside. Outside, I found the nest and it was a big one. It would have to be poisoned. I didn't get to hunt that morning, because of the search for the nest, and I knew I also smelled strongly of bug spray. I made a trip to town.

If you've never been the victim of a fire ant attack, you've never lived where they live. Fire ants burrow into the ground at least six feet. They haul all the tailings from their deep delving up to the surface and build a mound. There may be several mounds above one enormous underground nest. They are opportunistic feeders, and they swarm by the hundreds, even thousands, when agitated.

Every bite is slightly venomous, extremely painful and you can expect to be bitten multiple times. Small children, people with allergies and the elderly can be killed by them. They will kill and eat anything that doesn't escape from them, whether animal, vegetable, or me and you.

Which is why, later in the middle of the morning, I was at the feed store in Henderson, getting supplied with fire ant poison to apply to the nest, when my phone rang. I had no cell phone service out at the hunting lease.

"J.W. this is Christine. Can you come over to the apartment right away?"

I could hear tension in her voice.

"What's wrong?"

"Oh, nothing is wrong, J.W. I just need you to come over and talk with Lori and me."

I was alarmed. She knew I was going to be out at the hunting lease for the weekend.

"Well sure, Christine, but I'm in Henderson at the moment. I was planning to hunt later today. It will take me more than an hour to get there."

"I was afraid of that." She replied.

Why had she said she was afraid?

"Are you OK?"

"Yes, J.W., I just have a headache the size of an elephant. Get here as quickly as you can."

She hung up.

On the drive to Tyler I rolled the conversation over in my mind. The first thing ringing the alarm bells was she had said she was afraid, then used the phrase "the size of an elephant," Lori's danger code. We had chosen it as the phrase Lori would use if she ever felt she was in danger.

The second thing confirming the alarm was Christine had called me "J.W." She never called me J.W. Tony was the only person who did. Christine always called me John.

Calling me 'J.W.' might have been Christine's way of telling me we were going to need Tony's help.

Combining Lori's alarm code, along with her other language, indicated she and Lori were in serious danger.

After a brief stop at my apartment, I drove to Christine's apartment complex.

Tony met me just outside the parking lot, a couple of buildings away, and completely out of sight from Christine's apartment building. There were police cars, two ambulances, a fire truck, and the armored SWAT vehicle parked there.

"Man, I don't like this, J.W. I have guys in plainclothes observing her apartment. One of them went up the stairs and walked past her apartment. The door is closed, it appears to be undamaged, and all the blinds seem to be closed. With those reflective windows it's nearly impossible to see into an apartment in daylight anyway. If Orlando has found them, he's already inside the apartment. We don't have a clear view of the doorway from downstairs. We haven't been able to get a camera under the door. We have no idea what's happening inside her apartment." Tony was very agitated.

"Christine was clearly giving me a distress signal, Tony. They were in trouble when she called. I called back about thirty minutes ago, just to let them know I was on my way. She called me J.W. and urged me to 'hurry over, before she loses her mind'. I've never heard her say anything like that, before today."

"I understand, J.W., and I agree something is happening in there, but we don't know for sure what the exact nature of the threat is."

"Whatever it is, I'm going in." I said.

"Well then, I'm going with you." He replied.

"No. Whoever is in the apartment with Christine

and Lori is expecting me and me alone. It might spook him if he sees two people coming."

Tony shook his head. "You wouldn't let me go in there alone, J.W."

"We'll play it the way it's been presented. The people in the apartment are expecting me to be alone, so I will be. Tony, you can move in close and storm the place if there is any real trouble."

"J.W., I have the SWAT team staged near the building and standing by, ready to go. If you don't come out, with the girls, within five minutes, or if we hear shots or anything remotely suspicious, we're coming in."

"Thanks, Tony."

"You're welcome. Now don't go getting yourself killed. This Orlando cat is stupid and he's a dangerous dude. Once you're inside, we'll give you five minutes, J.W., not one second more, and then we're going to come in hot. Try to keep Orlando, or whoever it is, from looking out the windows." Tony instructed me.

"We don't know for sure who is in there with them, but I'll do my best." I said.

"Good luck."

"I don't believe in luck."

"Yeah, I know."

I got back in my truck, and drove the short distance to Christine's building. I parked just a few spaces away from the stairs leading to her floor. The parking space was directly outside her apartment. If anyone inside was watching for me, they would see me coming, but I couldn't see them because of the reflective windows on the building.

I was still dressed for hunting. I had on camouflage pants and a similar camo pattern, long sleeve shirt. I was carrying my camouflage jacket, tossed casually over one shoulder. I was even wearing a camo print ball cap. I had on my beat up old field boots.

I looked like hundreds of men and boys all over the country who were dressed the same way every weekend, in hunting season. In this part of the south, because we only hunt on private land, we don't have to wear blaze orange. Come to think of it, there are plenty of women who dress this way, or a variation of it, as well. At this time of year, a lot of us look like we belong in the cast of the TV show 'Duck Dynasty.'

I trotted up the stairs as if I didn't have a care in the world. When I reached Christine's door, it appeared undamaged, but there was a very clear, dirty tennis shoe print, right by the door knob and key lock. On closer examination, I could see the door had not been kicked open, but there was something odd going on. Christine would never have allowed a dirty shoe print on her door.

I took a deep breath.

I knocked on her door with the old familiar "shave and a haircut" beat.

A moment later, Christine called out, rather casually, "Come on in, it's open."

I turned the knob and opened the door into the entrance way.

Down the hall, in the living area, Walter peered around the corner and smiled.

He was holding Mr. Tumescence, Christine's cat."

"Yeah, buddy, come on in." Walter said.

When I stepped forward to go into the living area, something slammed into the back of my head, and the lights went out.

CHAPTER 40

"Hey, that's a cool gun," a voice said.

I opened my eyes to see Walter and Orlando both looking down at me.

I was lying on the floor just inside the living room. I guess Orlando must have dragged me in there, after he hit me. Walter was holding a Glock 19 in nine millimeter in his right hand, casually pointed at me. He had my .45 stuck in his waistband, and he was holding my Browning in his left hand. Clearly Walter had frisked me and found the guns I had been carrying under my shirt. My Jacket was lying in a chair where one of them had tossed it.

My head began to clear. There was a sharp pain all along the back of my head. I guessed Orlando had been behind the door when I came in, and had bashed me on the head with something. I had pretty much done the same thing to him, a few months ago.

Turn-about, is fair play.

I became aware of Christine and Lori, who were both seated side by side on the love seat, next to the couch.

Lori was holding Mr. Tumescence. She looked very sad. Christine looked angry.

"Gimme it," Orlando said, reaching out for my Browning as Walter was slipping it into his jacket pocket.

"Yes, I will, shortly. Right now I need you to help Mr. Tucker get on his feet. No, delete that... help him have a seat on the sofa."

After Orlando had shoved me onto the couch, Walter looked around the room at everyone and grinned.

"Now isn't this cozy, all the players in the same place, at the same time? I must say, I'm annoyed at you, Mr. Tucker. You've delayed the proceedings for far too long."

"What 'proceedings' did you have in mind, Walter?"

"Oh, I promised Orlando I would reunite him with Lori, among other things."

"Yeah, I can guess what those 'other things' are." I suggested.

"Well, Mr. Tucker, you're a clever boy. Let's hear what you think is going to happen."

"It's my belief your plan is that the only person who is going to leave here alive, is you."

"Oh, don't be so dramatic, Mr. Tucker. I am going to punish you. I'm going to start by having the date with Christine she has been so reluctant to do."

I looked at Christine.

She was staring calmly at Walter.

"Then, Orlando is going to have some fun with Lori."

I looked at Lori.

She was crying quietly, with big tears slowly running down her face.

"Walter, did you send one of your men to kill me?" I asked him.

"Yes, I did, and boy was I disappointed. It just goes to show, if you want something done right, you have to do it yourself."

"Why did you kill Ed Nordstrom?"

"You know why. It was just some routine house-keeping."

"No. I don't know why." I answered.

Walter's face got red.'

"Nordstrom was disloyal to me. That's why I killed him. Loyalty is a trait I value above all others. End of story."

I shook my head. "That's what your father says. It's not too late, Walter. You can stop all this and be forgiven. If you stop right now, we won't bring any charges against you."

"Oh, I wouldn't concern myself about such things, if I were you." He observed.

Walter took my .45 out of his waistband and handed it to Orlando.

"I think you'll find this is an even better gun than the one he stole from you. Keep it pointed at Mr. Tucker, and feel free to shoot him or Lori, if he so much as moves a hair."

Orlando grinned and jacked the slide on my .45, pointing it first at me, then Lori, back and forth. I knew as little as four pounds of pressure on the trigger would fire my gun. If he continued to wave it around, he was likely to kill one of us by accident.

"Get up Christine; we're going in the bedroom," Walter said, pointing his Glock at her.

Christine stood up very calmly and led the way into the bedroom. As she walked past me, she caught my eye and I saw something strong, something like confidence there.

"Don't do this Walter. The police will know you raped her." I warned him.

Walter paused in the doorway.

"You must think I'm stupid. I've been telling everyone for months, Christine is my girlfriend. The phone records will confirm it, and I've even brought my toothbrush. You see, I know how to plan ahead."

He closed the door behind him.

"Orlando, listen to me. Walter means to kill you, me, and both of the women," I said, desperately.

He grinned. "You, for sure, dude. Me? No, I don't think so."

"He's been planning this for months. It's why he hired an attorney to bail you out."

"Planning what?" Orlando asked, stupidly.

"He means to make himself look like a hero. He's going to kill you with his Glock. Then he's going to kill me, and both of these women, with the same gun you're holding right now. He'll make it look like he came here and found you, having just killed us. He'll be the big man who killed you."

"… Say what?"

It all happened at once.

From inside Christine's bedroom, there was the sound of three, fast gunshots. Inside the apartment, the noise was shocking and incredibly loud.

Orlando looked toward the bedroom, just as the front door crashed in. There was the sound of shattering glass in both of the bedrooms.

Orlando turned back toward the front door, swinging my .45 in that direction.

I shot him three times with his own stolen .38, which I had left hidden between the cushions of the couch, since the last time I had been here.

Orlando went down, like a balloon with all the air escaping.

Several armored SWAT team men came into the

room, all levelling their assault rifles on me.

I slowly set the .38 on the floor, and raised my hands high above my head.

"He's a friendly," Tony yelled, coming in behind them.

"Clear," someone yelled from inside the guest bedroom.

"Clear," someone yelled from Christine's bedroom.

"All Clear," Tony yelled, as he knelt beside Orlando, pocketing the .38.

I went to Lori. She had buried her face in Mr. Tum's fur. The cat had remained unruffled through the noise and violence. He was actually purring. Lori was sobbing.

I stroked her hair. "It's OK, baby girl. Everything is OK, now."

Christine's bedroom door opened and a heavily armed and armored SWAT team member led Christine into the living room. She looked perfectly calm.

"This lady dropped the perp back in there, sir, he's deader than disco," the armored officer said, pointing over his shoulder at Christine's bedroom.

"That guy had two guns, but she shot him three times, with this," he said, holding up Christine's "Judge" revolver. "When I came through the window, she nearly unloaded the last two on me. I was quick to take it away from her."

Tony was feeling for a pulse at Orlando's jugular vein.

"This one is still alive, call in the EMTs," Tony said, standing up. He was standing with one foot securing my .45.

I looked at Christine. She was beginning to tremble. I could tell she was starting to crumble.

Tony saw it too.

"Christine, come sit down here with Lori." Tony said, as he wrapped an arm around her. She collapsed against him and began to sob.

Tony embraced her and let her cry. With his foot, he slid my .45 away from where Orlando was curled on the carpet, which was slowly soaking up his blood. The stain resistant chemicals in the carpet fibers, like the four of us, being gradually overwhelmed.

CHAPTER 41

The SWAT team had used ladders at the end of the building to access the roof, and then simultaneously breeched the front door and rappelled through the bedroom windows of Christine's apartment.

I was sadly aware if I could have just convinced Walter not to follow through on his plans, or even delayed him just a moment or two longer, he might still be alive and Orlando might not be fighting for his life in the back of an ambulance on the way to the ER. If I had just walked up the stairs, instead of jogging… if this, if that…

"It is what it is." I thought I heard myself mumble.

There was something wrong with me.

My head hurt, horribly.

Christine was putting Mr. Tumescence into a cat carrier, so we could all be escorted out of the apartment which was now a crime scene.

The whole apartment seemed somehow too small now; there were too many heavily armed soldiers, and I couldn't see clearly.

When I tried to stand up, the room was swimming.

I had to sit down.

Tony was watching me and he called for the back-up EMTs.

"Well, J.W., this is what you get for not following my advice. If we had just breached the apartment without you going in, you wouldn't have gotten your bell rung,"

"No, Tony, they were watching for John at the window. There's no telling what would have happened if they had seen the police coming," Christine said.

She had "Tummy" in the carrier and was ready to go.

Lori stood with her. She had stopped crying. She was looking at me with a very concerned expression.

"It was a miracle it turned out this way, Tony. If I had been in town and could have gotten over here within minutes, there wouldn't have been time to get the SWAT team assembled and into position. Walter couldn't afford to have any gunfire in the apartment before I got here. He knew once gunshots were heard, the police would be on the way. In order for his plan to work, he had to make it look like he showed up and took out Orlando, just moments too late to save the women, and me. He wanted it to look like I had failed to protect Lori from Orlando, and my failure cost everyone their lives. He would emerge as the hero who protected Lori's parents and killed the bad guy. He got too cocky, I guess the recent attention we got in the press pushed his buttons." I said.

Then I threw up.

"Where are those medics?" Tony yelled.

"Coming up the stairs, LT," somebody said.

The light was hurting my eyes.

"Ladies, please come with me," A policeman said.

I was vaguely aware Lori was now sitting next to

me on the couch.

"No, not till I know he's OK," she said.

"I'll be fine, honey. You go on with Christine and Mr. Tumescence."

The EMTs showed up and checked me out.

"We need to get him to the ER. His pupils are unequally dilated. He may have a serious head injury."

The ride to the hospital in the ambulance was not fun. At the hospital, the ER staff was efficient, but all the examinations and tests took hours. Eventually I was diagnosed with a moderate concussion, with no skull fracture.

I would fully recover, other than the permanent minimal brain damage. No worries, some people figure I'm brain damaged anyway.

They decided to keep me overnight for observation. It was nearly dark outside by the time I was put into a bed in a hospital room.

Christine had come to the hospital at some point.

She found me in my room. She sat in one of those odd, futon–like hospital chairs that double as a recliner, for family or friends to sleep on.

"Lori is with her parents now. The police took us downtown to give statements, and her parents met us there. Tony said you could come in and give your statement whenever you feel up to it." Christine informed me.

"Not today."

"Well, maybe not officially, but Tony came with me, and he'll be here any minute."

I closed my eyes.

"Hey, J.W. Long day, huh?" Tony asked, as he walked into the room.

I squinted at him.

"I woke up with fire ants,"

He and Christine looked at each other and then both of them looked at me, with some concern clearly evident on their faces. My statement seemed strange to them. I guess they figured I was deranged.

I started to chuckle, but it made my head hurt, even worse.

"This morning, in my trailer, I had fire ants in my sleeping bag. I was at the hunting lease, remember?"

They both looked relieved.

"Ouch," Tony said.

"Yeah, but if they hadn't been there, I wouldn't have gotten Christine's phone call," I said.

"God sent the ants," Christine said.

I shrugged.

"I know He did, John. I felt Him with me, through this whole day. I prayed and He… It's as if… I met Jesus today."

"Yeah, you nearly did," Tony said.

"No, Tony, I really did!" She was beaming. "I met Jesus today! He gave me peace and it was as if I were being bathed in light, and there was this… I can't really describe it."

I grinned. "You don't have to. I knew there was something different about you."

Tony was staring at Christine.

He nodded. "Yeah, I see it too. I guess it explains how well you've managed, after…" He trailed off.

"Oh, I'm so very, very… sad, about Walter. He looked so… surprised." she said dejectedly.

"I'm sorry too, Christine, he made his own choices," I said.

She bowed her head.

"After, when the policeman brought me out of the room, I looked at his body. It was just an empty husk. Walter wasn't there anymore." She closed her eyes. "I don't ever want to have to do something like that again."

Tony reached over and took Christine's hand; he sat on the arm of her chair.

We sat in silence for a while.

Eventually, I asked, "Is Lori OK?"

"Yes, John. She was just so overcome with shame and sadness. She couldn't believe she had ever thought there was anything good or attractive about either Orlando or Walter. She told me when she saw Orlando hit you, it broke her heart. She felt responsible. She felt responsible for all of it. She was horribly worried about you. I called her the minute we heard the diagnosis," Christine replied.

"Good thing I have such a hard head, huh?"

"Humph! Thick maybe, so thick there's probably barely room for your pea brain." Tony said.

Christine still wanted to talk about Lori.

"I'm trying to help Lori understand none of this was directly her fault. What happened with her and Orlando, happened because of choices she made, and she experienced the consequences of those choices. She's made better choices since, and all that went before is just water under the bridge. Everything Walter was a part of was always and only, all about Walter."

"How is Orlando?" I asked.

"He'll live to stand trial, despite your remarkable shooting skills. Somehow, even with a concussion and sitting on a couch, you managed to hit him three times with three shots. You put him down, but the medics got him stabilized and he's had some surgery. He's right here in this hospital, in guarded condition," Tony responded.

"It's not too late for him. He can still repent and choose redemption." I said.

Tony made a sort of 'who knows' gesture.

We were aware, for some people the only time or place they ever hear the gospel, is when they are in jail. It was possible that Orlando would go into prison as a prisoner of the devil, and come out of prison with new freedom in Christ.

Christine was struggling with something.

"John, do you know why they didn't... why didn't they... you know... Why didn't Walter and Orlando rape us, in the hour we were waiting for you to get there?"

"Why do you think?" I asked her.

Christine glanced at Tony, then back at me.

"I've thought about it a lot. I think Walter thought it would hurt you more, if you were there when it happened. It would make him feel more powerful and in control. He wanted to show you what he was capable of, and that you couldn't do anything about it."

I nodded. "I expect the whole thing was about him trying to prove to himself he was powerful and in control."

"Yeah, and that he was smarter than all of us," Tony added. "He thought he could get away with rape and murder, as if there were no justice."

"As if he thought there was no God," Christine added.

I sighed.

"He knows better now."

CHAPTER 42

Tony came to pick me up from the hospital on Sunday morning.

I felt silly being wheeled out of the hospital in a wheelchair, all decked out in camouflage on a Sunday morning. Maybe I was dressed to go to the church in the wild wood. Actually, that's my favorite kind of church. I was holding my cap in my hands. My head hurt too much to consider wearing it, until the sun blazed into my eyes. I immediately draped the cap loosely over my eyes.

"Thanks, for picking me up, Tony. Sorry you have to miss church to run this errand."

"No problem, J.W. I'm happy to do it. Your truck is still parked in the lot outside Christine's apartment; do you feel up to driving?"

"No, I barely got any sleep last night. They kept waking me up to check on me. They really didn't want me to sleep at all, so much for my plans to enjoy a weekend of solitude in the wilderness. I'm ready for a hot shower, and a nap."

"At least now you can put all this Walter Farley business behind you."

"I never wanted it to end like this. I wish he

would have made better choices."

"I know, J.W., me too. He was one twisted off individual. I guess I'll have to put the Nordstrom case down as 'unsolved', even though we both know Walter probably did it."

"Walter told me he did it."

Yeah, so you and the women say, but there's no way to prove it."

"We'll see about that."

"What do you mean?"

"Where is my jacket?"

"What jacket? You mean the camouflage jacket you were wearing in the parking lot? I forgot all about it. I guess it's still at the crime scene. You weren't wearing it when we came in."

"Yeah, that's the one. I last saw it on a chair in Christine's living room. In one of the pockets of my jacket, is my cell phone. I left it on, in the 'record memo' application. Odds are it will have recorded everything that happened in the room, including Walter admitting he killed Nordstrom."

Tony shook his head.

"I don't know, J.W. It seems unlikely. Wouldn't Walter have noticed it?"

"Maybe, maybe not, we'll see. In the meantime, we should have some pretty interesting video."

"… Video?"

"Yep, you see, it's a process of recording events, using a motion picture video camera."

Tony scowled at me.

"I know what it is, J.W. I just don't know how there could be a video. There were no cameras in Christine's apartment. When I asked her, she verified it."

I reached into my shirt pocket.

"Write this down…" I said, trying to hand him my pen.

"I'm driving, you numbskull. You write it down."

I chuckled, and it didn't hurt too badly.

"Tony this pen has a digital video camera built into it. I've had it clipped into my shirt pocket, and they didn't take it away from me. It should have some pretty interesting footage. I'm afraid I don't have a clear memory of exactly how well I used my body to frame the shots, but there will be something useful there."

"… No way!"

"Way."

I spent the rest of Sunday watching football on TV and snoozing, off and on.

Monday morning I arrived at work bright and early, at about ten o'clock. I figured it was pretty early, given the weekend I had.

I was surprised to see Christine at her desk. She wasn't surprised to see me. She saw me on the monitor as I was exiting the elevator.

I was more surprised to see Mr. Tumescence in the office. He was curled up in my chair, behind my desk.

I raised my eyebrows at Christine.

"I just couldn't stand the thought of Tummy being boarded with the vet for one more day. I'm staying at a motel that allows pets, but I didn't expect to see you today, so I brought him with me."

"I thought I told you to take a few days off, while I recuperate,"

"I know, but somebody has to deal with the phones. Do you plan to recuperate while you work?"

"Uh, I just thought I would come in and check the answering machine." I fibbed.

"Yeah, right, we have an answering service. Have you seen the news?"

"No, I pretty much only watch football, I watched enough TV yesterday to last me till tonight. Monday night football, you know!"

"… Really? I'm pretty sure I've seen you watch CNN and the local news. I know you watch movies. I guess you haven't seen a newspaper either."

I shook my head, carefully.

Christine shook hers too. "As you may imagine, a SWAT team storming an apartment in Tyler, with shots fired, has gotten a lot of attention."

"Oh no," I said.

"Oh yes. You and Tony are famous again. The phone has been ringing off the hook."

The newspaper told the story of how on a tip from a citizen, the Tyler police SWAT team had stormed an apartment where two area women were being held hostage. In the carefully coordinated rescue, one armed suspect was killed and another seriously wounded. None of the hostages were harmed. The SWAT team was under the command of Detective Lieutenant Tony Escalante of the Tyler Police Department's Robbery/Homicide Division.

When asked for a comment, Lieutenant Escalante stated, "We are generally pleased at the outcome of this action, though we regret the loss of life."

The reporter had also learned one of the suspects was a man currently out on bail, awaiting trial on a previous burglary and home invasion charge, possession of controlled substances, and charges related to an assault on a police officer in College Station. The suspect who died was also a suspect in a homicide that had occurred in Tyler, earlier in the year. The citizen who alerted the police was the celebrated local private investigator, John Wesley Tucker.

I was thankful the women had not been named at all in the story.

The next story on the front page, below the fold, was about the noted Tyler oil and gas magnate and entrepreneur, Ted Simpson. He was announcing his intention to run for the office of Governor of the State of Texas.

CHAPTER 43

"Do you have an appointment, Mr. Tucker?"

The Simpson Oil and Gas Company now had a receptionist on the ground floor. There was also a security stop with a baggage scanner and a metal detector. It looked like what you might expect to see at any corporate headquarters.

"No, ma'am, I don't. However, if he's in, I expect he'll want to see me. Otherwise, I'll make an appointment."

She picked up the phone and talked for a moment.

"He's in a meeting this morning. We'll have to contact you with an appointment time. Do you have a card?"

"Yes, ma'am, I do."

I gave her my card and left the building. Just as well, I would have had to leave my gun in the truck anyway.

The call came in about thirty minutes later.

"Tucker, can you come down here? I need to talk to you privately. I'll buy you lunch."

"Yes sir. I can meet you for lunch. Where would you like to meet?"

"Come on down here to the Simpson building. We'll talk first, and then we'll eat."

He hung up.

When I met him in his office, he was seated at his desk.

"Sit down, Tucker, I don't have time for small talk, so I'll get to the point. I guess you know I've announced my bid for Governor."

"Yes sir. The timing of your announcement was... interesting."

"What I do and when I do it, is none of your damn business. That's the point. I expect you to keep your mouth shut. You've hurt me bad enough, but I'm willing to let bygones be bygones, if you are?"

"What do you have in mind?" I asked.

He leaned back in his chair and looked up at the ceiling.

"Would a hundred thousand dollars buy your silence?"

I sighed.

"No sir."

He shot me an angry look.

I held my hands up.

"Hear me out, Mr. Simpson. I don't want your money. I have no intention of telling anyone about your relationship with Walter Farley. I'm a private investigator; I don't divulge anything about my client's. Not even former clients like yourself. I consider the matter closed. However, sir; the thing is this, if I found out about Walter and his relationship to you, someone else can do the same work I did, and reach the same conclusions."

He shook his head. "Nope, I don't expect that will happen. As far as the whole world knows, Walter was just my personal assistant. He had some kind of weird attraction to a former employee, but I had no knowledge of it. I'll see to it the few people who know any different are paid to keep their mouths shut."

I gave him a skeptical look.

"Walter owned World Wide Security Agency outright. There is no connection to me personally, nothing of record about me providing the start-up capital. Sure, Simpson Oil and Gas hired WWSA to provide some security services, but I'll swear we didn't know Walter owned that outfit. I'll just claim he tricked us, the same way he tricked everybody else." He said smugly.

"Mr. Simpson, I don't think there is any chance you'll get away with this. I think it will stick to you like a bad smell. Your son isn't even buried yet, and you're acting as if you never knew him. Walter stole industrial technology for you. He killed at least one man, for nothing more than disloyalty. If Walter was loyal to you, and you value loyalty so much, where is your loyalty to him?"

"That's water under the bridge. He's gone and that's that."

"Do you really believe you can become Governor through deception and bribery?

He chuckled. "Hell yes, boy! Don't you know anything about politics?"

I was shielding my eyes from the overhead lights.

"You alright, Tucker? You don't look too good."

"It's just a headache, sir. This whole business makes me sick."

"Well, how do you think I feel? My only son was killed, because of you."

I took a deep breath. "No sir, that's not true. Your son Walter died because of the choices he made. He could have chosen differently. He just wanted to be big and powerful. Like his father."

That silenced him, for a moment.

"OK, boy, here's the deal. I have a non-disclosure document our attorneys drew up. I want you to sign it. It basically states if you ever divulge any of this to anyone, or if we even think you might have, we'll own you, your business, and your future, forever. You sign it, and I'll cut you a check for two hundred and fifty thousand dollars."

I sat thoughtfully for a moment. Then I stood up.

"Mr. Simpson, when I came in here, I told you I didn't want your money, and I had no intention of talking about this to anyone. Now you've offered me a quarter of a million dollars to buy my silence. It's something to think about. Let me think about this deal for an hour or so. OK?"

He narrowed his eyes at me.

"Fine, I'll give you one hour, but the price is non-negotiable. Let's get us some lunch."

He stood up.

"No thank you, sir, I really do have a headache and I don't feel well. I need to take a walk and get some air."

"Fine, it's a beautiful fall day in East Texas. I'll see you when you get back. Believe me, boy; this is good business, good for both of us. If you don't take the deal, it will be very bad for you."

I left his office, without shaking his hand.

When I got outside on the side walk, I looked around the square. It really was a beautiful day in East Texas. The sun was shining through the brightly colored leaves that still remained on the trees, and the fountain was splashing and twinkling in the light. I took a deep breath and turned my face up toward the sun.

I enjoyed my walk across the square, to the building that housed the local ABC network television affiliate.

Ten minutes later, I was showing the video of my meeting with Ted Simpson, which I had filmed with my new "pen cam" firmly clipped into my shirt pocket, to the news director and others. They seemed to think it was newsworthy. We discussed the possibility of me giving an on-camera interview, which I declined. I insisted I not be named as the source of the video, and that my name be edited out. I knew it was possible someone might recognize my voice, but there would be no way to positively identify me. The media circus would be focused on Ted Simpson. It might even be a pretty entertaining circus.

Exactly one hour after I had left his office, I called Mr. Simpson on his private line and rejected his offer.

His disappointment was as palpable as his avarice and ambition.

EPILOGUE

Most people lead lives of solitary anxiety, solitary, because they don't talk about their fears with anyone. They don't even want to admit that they have them.

They don't know who they are, or why they are on the earth.

Introspection only brings more doubts and fears, so they seek solace from science.

Science tells them that they are just biological organisms, evolved from muck, eking out a brief existence at the expense of a doomed planet. Science tells them that life is random, meaningless and pointless. Take another pill, and try not to think about it.

The clock is ticking.

Many, wander through life aimlessly waiting for the clock to run out. Some are seeking to find something that makes them feel as if their life matters in some way. They mostly want to "do the right thing," but violently disagree on what "right" is, because, "Every way of a man is right, in his own eyes."

The clock is ticking.

People know that from the moment of birth, they are doomed. They know that life is short and uncertain. It may end at any time. The best of them ask "why"?

Why do we exist? Why are we the way we are? Why do bad things happen? Why is there suffering and death? What happens after we die? Do we just cease to exist? When we die, will it be as if we had never existed at all? Why?

The world offers many different and conflicting answers. Most of them are lies.

So, most people everywhere, in every walk of life, are as lost as sheep without a shepherd, stumbling blindly through however many days that remain to them, silently screaming in desperation.

The clock is ticking.

I know why I get up in the morning. I know what I'm supposed to do and how I should do it. I live to serve, but I don't serve the planet earth, the government, or myself.

I serve the holy God; the creator of all things. I am appointed as one of His ambassadors in this place.

I serve The Good Shepherd.

He alone is perfect.

His sheep are imperfect, but His sheep know His voice when they hear it.

Other sheep wander around lost, following whatever voice sounds most pleasant to them at the moment, even the voices that lead them to slaughter.

Sheep without a shepherd are helpless against the predators.

I am appointed as a Shepherd of His sheep, to seek the lost sheep, and to stand against the wolves.

We who serve as Shepherds are also imperfect, but we are empowered and equipped for service.

I have the sword of Truth, the message of glorious hope.

I have work to do.

I wish I were a better Shepherd.

The clock is ticking.

ACKNOWLEDGEMENTS

Thanks to Liz Quinn, for being my beta reader and first editor. In addition to the usual copy editing, she suggested some changes that were spot on. Thank you, Liz.

I want to thank Carol Cassella, author of Gemini, Healer, and Oxygen. Carol encouraged me and advised me on matters related to publishing. Thank you, Carol.

May God bless all of you.

Whatever errors there are in the execution of this book are entirely my own.

A LOOK AT: SPECIAL AGENT (ANGELS & IMPERFECTION 2)

HIS SERVICE TO OTHERS IS NOT JUST WORK, BUT A CALLING, AND NO PRICE IS TOO HIGH.

When a young man is forced into hiding after rescuing a helpless woman from the leader of a vicious street gang, private investigator John Wesley Tucker is sent to find him.

Tucker finds himself in need of help from an old friend, who also has need of John's help. The two friends work together to save the young man from the hit squad sent to kill him, culminating in a firefight in the belly of a cypress bayou. The young man learns there is more to life than just living.

Tucker's other cases include attempting to apprehend the killer of an undocumented immigrant, investigating the hidden agenda of a federal agent, and attempting to thwart a domestic terrorist attack. Soon he learns these cases are all connected. When the FBI raids an old farmhouse, many people die in the flames.

Only Tucker knows what really happened, will he stay alive long enough to expose the secret?

Coming May 2020

ABOUT THE AUTHOR

Born in Bakersfield, California and abandoned by his parents in Seattle, Washington. After living in the foster care system for some years, Dan Arnold was eventually adopted. He's traveled internationally, lived in Idaho, Washington, California, Virginia, and now makes his home in Texas with his wife Lora. They have four grown children and three grandchildren of whom they are justifiably proud, not because they are such good parents, but because God is good.

A Member of the Association of Christian Fiction Writers, and Western Writers of America, in 2015, writing under the name Daniel Roland Banks, his book Angels & Imperfections was selected as a finalist in Christian Fiction in the Reader's Favorite International Book awards.

Find more great titles by Dan Arnold and Christian Kindle News at https://christiankindlenews. com/our-authors/dan-arnold/